Life Study with Dead Body

The Monterey Peninsula art world is the background for private investigator Patrick Riordan's brush with death, as he stumbles across the nude, blood-covered body of a promising young painter in her Carmel cottage. On an easel nearby stands an oil painting which exactly depicts the murder scene—and which the artist has neglected to sign.

Riordan and his feisty sidekick Reiko chase clues from the galleries and boutiques of Carmel to bohemian studios in Big Sur to the moneyed world of Pebble Beach. The solution? An immutable condition, an inevitable conclusion:

D0865592

Chinese Restaurants Never Serve Breakfast

Roy Gilligan

Chinese Restaurants Never Serve Breakfast

A *mystery from*
Perseverance Press
MENLO PARK, CALIFORNIA

Art direction by Gary Page/Merit Media.
Photography by Rob Egashira/Fabrizio Camera Graphics.
Paintings by Reed Farrington, author's collection.
Typography by Jim Cook.

Published by

Perseverance Press
P.O. Box 384
Menlo Park, California 94026

Manufactured in the United States of America.

1 2 3 — 88 87 86

Library of Congress Catalog Card Number: 86-60391

ISBN: 0-9602676-4-6

For Jane and the D.K.

And, of course, for Mayor Eastwood.

The author is deeply indebted to Reed Farrington, whose voluptuous nude, on the cover, inspired the writing of this book, and whose portrait of the author, back cover, makes him look more mysterious than he deserves.

Chinese Restaurants Never Serve Breakfast

HELEN AND I were together for a long time, and we had a lot of little private things—jokes, phrases, cryptic sayings—that were special to us.

Whenever we recognized that we had come across an immutable condition or arrived at an inevitable conclusion, we'd look at each other and one of us would say, "Well, Chinese restaurants never serve breakfast."

It's an immutable condition that Helen is dead.

And the case of Sheila Lord reached an inevitable conclusion.

And Nancy Blanchard's secret isn't a secret any more.

And a woman I think I could have loved is gone from me forever.

There's no tragedy here. It's just the way things are.

Chinese restaurants never serve breakfast.

1

My life has been filled with demurring.

A TALL SKINNY man in faded gray coveralls is lettering my name on that frosted glass door. His depth of concentration is marvelous to watch. Painfully, he measured the exact dimensions of his project and drafted the letters with a watchmaker's precision. Now he is filling in the lines with opaque black paint. Never does his hand allow the brush to waver. Michelangelo working on the Sistine Chapel.

I sit back on a brand new foam-padded swivel chair and watch the name materialize across the glass from right to left backwards. There is a comfortable warm feeling glowing inside me. I have done what I have been promising myself to do for too many years. I have taken an office, one and a half rooms over a bakery, on Alvarado Street in Monterey. After too many years in San Francisco, I have removed my middle-aged body and my business to my favorite place in the Pacific West. All that remains to be seen is whether I can make a living here.

When the sign is finished, the name on the door will be Patrick J. Riordan. Beneath it will be the modest legend "Private Investigations." Reiko, my right arm and sometime keeper, suggested that I use something rakish and Bogartian: "The Monterey Eye." But I demurred. My life has been filled with demurring. Time after time, I'd talked myself out of the move I have just made. I had wanted desperately to settle on the Monterey Peninsula. But, no, San

Francisco was the only place for a private investigator. Anybody knows that. Any *Maltese Falcon* fan knows that. I knew that.

Throughout the twenty years I spent in San Francisco, I fantasized that I was following in the footsteps of Hammett and Bogie, sauntering through the fog in a snapbrim and a trench coat, following exotic women and patently evil men. What I actually *did*, however, was trail around after dumb husbands who were obsessed with afternoon fornication and thought they could get away with it. I chased down wives who took off their rings in singles bars and searched for the past in younger men. It was depressing.

Oh, there were cases other than the unfaithful spouse act. I worked for lawyers (even Belli, the old sonofabitch), gathering evidence for some pretty interesting criminal trials. I knew a guy who could run a polygraph. I had quite a few clients in that electronic Disneyland fifty miles to the south known as Silicon Valley. That's a hotbed of industrial and international espionage; those people are constantly stealing secrets and vice presidents from each other. Now and then a trusted employee peddles vital information—and sometimes his life—through a broker to some foreign power. Those poor bastards are amateurs and pretty easy to catch.

For some reason, a lot of my business has come from the rich, obscure, and discreet. People who have frequent problems and lots of money to pay somebody to solve them. People who have names that they want kept out of the paper. In a way, that's why I'm in Monterey now.

I didn't have it so bad in San Francisco. I could pay Reiko most of the time, and I kept busy. But the Monterey Peninsula has always been my place of refuge and respite. I came here every chance I had. Something drew me. The air is better. It could be my imagination, but people seem to be just a bit happier. And the scenery in all directions is magnificent. I even love the fog that the summer tourists invariably complain about.

Over the years, I had acquired a certain number of clients on the Peninsula, mostly in Pebble Beach. They were all people of inestimable wealth who kept places in San Francisco or Marin County or Hillsborough as well as getaway *pieds-à-terre* in Pebble

Beach or Malibu. I had handled divorce investigations and runaways and other unmentionable annoyances for these people in all their locations, and once in a while one would call me in the city and demand my presence for an assignment here. As a matter of fact, that's how this whole move came about.

For ten or twelve years, I have been working steadily—at regular intervals—for a guy I shall call George Spelvin. (It's a show-biz name, plugged into the program when the actor hasn't been cast at press time, or wants to remain unidentified. There's a female who works in porno films who's been calling herself Georgina Spelvin, but she won't be around much longer. Those women all fade away when their boobs begin to droop.) Anyway, I don't want to use George's real name because the family has a pedigree that would run to two or three volumes. Good old George, now in his early sixties, has a weakness for marriage. Maybe it's the ceremony, the church, and the flowers. Maybe he likes the words, although he must have them committed to memory by now. He has always insisted on the big production under stained glass, with a modest reception for five hundred. And he has always married beautiful young tramps, all of whom have separated him from a chunk of the principal and departed smiling. I had known five of them, and there might have been others. However, his latest one was different. She was special. But I'm going to tell you all about her. Wait a minute, I'm not sure I know *all* about her.

George was responsible for my socialite connections. He was drunk the first time he ever called me, in San Francisco years ago. Just got my number out of the yellow pages by opening the book to the right section, closing his eyes, and jabbing his finger. He was also responsible for my move to Monterey.

"I need you, Riordan," he said on the phone last July.

"So I'll be down, George. In a couple of days. Hang in there."

He sounded sober and more urgent than usual.

"I need you bad, baby. Look, you told me you're pretty fed up with San Francisco, right? You would like to live down here, right? Your business isn't that good in San Francisco. I know that. Besides, the city ain't what it used to be. It's crowded and smelly and dirty and it's got all those goddam ugly buildings. I need you here, Riordan."

He was right. My business in San Francisco had been diminishing over the years. And my rent, even in one of the oldest buildings on Market Street, was spiraling into the blue yonder. It is true that I had always yearned to live on the Monterey Peninsula. And George had pressed the right button.

"What's your proposition, George?"

"Come on down and we'll talk. Meet me at the Lodge tomorrow for lunch. Noonish. I'll be in the bar."

It was about four in the afternoon. I told Reiko not to expect me in the morning and she just snorted. I grabbed a cable car to my flat on Russian Hill, packed a few appropriate things, and took off for Monterey.

Next day we were sitting in the bar at the Lodge in Pebble Beach, both sipping Perrier and lime. This was not George's usual drink. He was still sober and serious. It was one of those blindingly bright summer days that occur infrequently in July.

When I could tear my gaze from the unbelievably blue Pacific across the eighteenth green of one of the world's greatest golf courses, I looked at my host over the tiny table. A very trim sixty-two he was, aging slowly and gracefully, like Cary Grant. George was not especially tall, but his slenderness gave him an illusory inch or two. He never wore a tie, and his expensively tailored sports shirts never had a reptile—or beast of any kind—pasted on the left breast. His razor-creased slacks were beltless, and his Guccis soft and light as air. The most obvious signs of his affluence were the necklace he always wore, a large gold scarab on a gold chain with links as big as dimes, and the heavy gold Rolex that seemed to dangle from his slender wrist.

George Spelvin is a handsome man, deep-tanned and silver-haired. It's no wonder those empty-headed chickies were genuinely attracted to him. But he has the look of the patrician society drunk: permanent pouches under his light blue eyes and a nose covered with tiny blood vessels which he tries to cover with after-shave power. The well-trimmed mustache does not conceal the sensual mouth, and the movie-star smile is by the best cosmetic dentist in Beverly Hills.

"Riordan," George said as he sipped some Perrier and deftly

removed a wisp of lime pulp from his teeth, "I know you like it here. And I owe you something more than dollars for being so goddam patient with me for these many years. I know that you have a number of clients scattered around Monterey County. I can get you more, most of whom have more problems—and money—than I have."

George was struggling a little. He had something heavy on his mind.

"I'm married again, you know."

I didn't—until that moment.

"This one's different, Pat. I'm afraid—"

There was pain in his face, and he averted his eyes. I looked out the window and watched a guy blow a three foot putt on eighteen.

"You want me to check her out, George? I don't have to move my business down here for that."

He composed himself. "It's just that I think we can—excuse the expression—kill two birds with one stone. I can do a little something for you, and you...can do a pretty big something for me.

"What I'm going to propose, Pat, is that you take my little house in Carmel—rent free, of course—and find an office somewhere. Monterey would be your best bet. You can move your operation down here and even bring that little Chinese girl—"

"Japanese," I said, automatically.

"Whatever," said George. "You can bring her and settle here and be happy. And you can help me. I suspect you won't lose a nickel. How about it?"

"What about my Silicon Valley clients?"

"For Christ's sake, Riordan, the way they're crashing up there and eating each other up, you might not have any in a little while. Besides, they're all just about an hour away if you go through Santa Cruz. You'll live here free. You can paint when you want to. And this little house is a gem. It's all furnished and just a block off upper Ocean. I kept it for...guests. And some friends who always come down for the golf tournaments. But they can go to hell. They always messed up the place anyhow."

I knew that George had kept that little house for years. I knew why he kept it. As we sat in the bar at the Lodge that day, it occurred to me that George had forgotten that on several occasions he had asked me to dislodge a tenant—gently but firmly. Each time I would rap the rusty knocker on the door of this fairy-tale cottage on Santa Rita Street and persuade a pretty young woman to depart by pressing in her hand an envelope whose contents I never examined and did not question. Never was there an argument. These were George's transient flings. It was the ones he married that caused all the trouble.

"When can I move in?"

"Hell, Riordan, any time. Today, tomorrow, next week. Place is always ready. Gets cleaned up once a week whether it needs it or not. Has telephones and cable TV hook-ups upstairs and down. Refrigerator's a little noisy—"

"George, I accept. But I'm too old for game playing. You better not be giving me a lot of bullshit."

The smooth, tan face broke into a big smile that revealed the heavy, natural lines that collagen injections had not been able to erase.

"Honest to God, Pat. This is me—ol' George. I've never lied to you."

His face darkened suddenly. "I need you, Pat. This...may be the last time. But I need you bad. I...don't want this one to get away. I've never been in a spot like this before."

George became businesslike: "If you want, Riordan, we'll put it in writing. You write it, I'll sign it."

But I was past the negotiating stage. George and I solemnly shook hands and the deal was made. I promised to call him in a couple of days and we parted with a clear understanding.

I was on the Seventeen Mile Drive, approaching the Pacific Grove gate, but my mind was miles away. The landlord of my flat on Russian Hill owed me one, at least. He'd let me break the lease anytime. Besides, he could rent the place for twice what I was paying him. And I wouldn't be around to remind him of some embarrassing family connections in North Beach.

The only real problem (I thought) was Reiko. She had been my anchor to reality for nearly nine years now, ever since Helen was killed. She had come into my office one day looking for a job and stayed on as assistant, bookkeeper, and confidante. Later she became much more—but when I suggested marriage, she backed off very quickly and firmly. Marriage to somebody "un-Japanese," she said, would cause her mother terrible pain. No matter how many times I tried, I couldn't get around that one. Mama was only a few years older than I am and in robust health.

But would Reiko accept the move? Whenever I made any suggestions about rearranging the office or the system, the hooded eyes became mere black slits, and she would glide sideways from me and change the subject.

I called her from a pay phone on Del Monte Avenue in Monterey as I was heading back to the city.

"How are things, Reiko-san?"

"Terrible. The bills need to be paid. You have six urgent phone messages. You missed an appointment with your dentist. And your dirty laundry is still in the bag under your desk. How's the weather?"

"Great. Sunshine, sea breeze. Hey, you want to live down here?"

Get right to the point, Riordan, with your fingers crossed.

"Sure, Pat. When do we leave? Shall I say anything to the building manager? Our lease runs to September, you know."

I smiled into the smelly phone. "Hey, you weren't supposed to react like that. I'm serious. George Spelvin has offered me a hell of an opportunity."

"Yes, I know. He called me ten minutes ago. Even offered to buy off our lease here. I just talked to my cousin Sandy in Pacific Grove, and she has a little apartment lined up for me. You've got to get in touch with my Uncle Shiro who owns an office building in Monterey. Riordan, are you listening?"

Reiko's far-flung family. It's all so easy.

Why do we always sweat the little things?

Or the inevitable conclusions?

2

George was pretty well juiced...

So IT's SEPTEMBER and we've been here since July. It was a hell of a summer.

I'm living in George's little house in Carmel. Reiko has a small apartment off Lighthouse in Pacific Grove. The man is painting the name on the office door. And the brand new furniture is all here. Reiko insisted that we dump everything but the files and get new stuff. And although Uncle Shiro had offered us some things out of his storeroom, she would have none of it. A new start is a new start.

As I said in the beginning, there is a foam padded swivel chair. There is also a desk the size of a Ping-Pong table, on which rests a telephone and a new phone book for Monterey and San Benito counties. In the half-room beyond a flimsy partition are my battered and scarred file cabinets from San Francisco and a tatami mat that Reiko occasionally sits on when she gets tired of the Norwegian-designed backless chair we bought for her desk. We now have a computer (which Reiko insisted upon). It's one of the best on the market and has all the trimmings. It has placed us heavily in debt. To date, however, Reiko has been able to handle all our business on a lined yellow pad attached to a clipboard. I have made a mental note that I might sell the computer and get her an abacus.

The tatami mat, however, was not Reiko's idea, as appropriate as it might seem. It's a souvenir from the Spelvin case. I swiped it, if you really want to know.

I am delighted with the Carmel house. It's one of the original Hansel-and-Gretel cottages that Hugh Comstock built in the late twenties. The ground floor is airy and uncluttered, with a large living room dominated by a natural stone fireplace and, through an arch, a dining area and kitchen. The floor is laid with eight-inch square terra cotta tiles in the rustic French manner, a real boon to a fairly sloppy bachelor. A narrow staircase leads to the bathroom and the large bedroom with a vaulted ceiling. Much has been done to the house, of course, since 1928. But it retains the essential charm of Carmel, a quality seriously eroded in recent years by commerce and avarice.

About Reiko's tatami mat. It isn't especially different from other tatami mats, although it's probably better made and thicker. It's about three feet by six, made up of intricately woven squares laced together. Nothing that would catch the eye. But it conjures up lots of visions for me, particularly involving a surprisingly sentimental killer on a dark night in a big house on Carmel Point.

I said I'd talk about George Spelvin's most recent wife. Maybe I've been avoiding it up to now. There is a residue of pain from that one. I allowed myself to become vulnerable.

Maybe you've already concluded that I am not your hard-drinking, fist-fighting, jump-in-the-sack-with-anybody kind of private eye. At least, not any more. You're right. Helen and I had a good marriage for fourteen years. We got along very well most of the time. We only yelled at each other about once a week. We had no kids. She was a buyer at I. Magnin and would be gone for several weeks at a time. I would be away on assignments in various parts of California and the other coastal states. We had it worked out. I never played around, and I'm quite sure she didn't.

Then one night we were driving up Highway 280 into San Francisco from a party (her friends, not mine) in Burlingame. It was about one a.m., and a drunk came across the divider at eighty miles an hour and killed my wife. I still cannot remember what happened. When I opened my eyes and saw the flashing lights and the cops and the paramedics, I was lying on the road with a broken arm and a deep gash in the head. They were loading Helen's body into a white van. I never saw her again. I was still in the hospital when she was cremated with no services, strictly according to her wishes.

That was ten years ago. When I met Debbie Spelvin last July in Pebble Beach, I'm afraid something happened to me that I had never expected to happen. But I'm over it now. I think.

Reiko and I had accomplished the move in record time. I moved into George's furnished house, Reiko's cousin had her apartment ready, and Uncle Shiro was more than helpful with an office that was perfect for us. We camped out for a while. In the beginning, in July, all we had was a telephone and a couple of chairs that looked like they might have seen service under the Mexican flag. We had left everything in San Francisco with instructions for the shipment of the file cabinets. We were, in a pretty shaky way, in business. In just about three days.

When we got settled, I called George. It was evident when he answered that he had been drinking, probably for several hours. He asked me to meet him at the Lodge. I got into my little Mercedes— an extravagance bought out of the insurance money after Helen's death—and headed for Pebble Beach.

George was pretty well juiced when I met him, more seriously disturbed than I had ever seen him before. He was rambling about his latest wife, a lady he described as being thirty-fivish and blonde and too goddam smart. But I could tell he was concerned, really worried. He kept telling me that she was trying to poison him with something in the hollandaise or was sexually involved with three local bartenders (one at a time, he carefully explained, with dignity)—or, maybe both the poison *and* the bartenders.

"Shit, Riordan, she's the best I ever had!"

I couldn't tell if he meant sex or companionship.

"She's a lady, goddammit!" he answered as his eyes welled up with tears.

I promised George that I would check out his wife's social life and report back. Forget about the hollandaise—it all tastes like that. Don't worry, though, George. First thing in the morning, George, first thing in the morning.

I left him staring into space at the bar and drove out through the

Carmel gate. It was still bright on that midsummer evening, a glorious fog-free day with the ocean breeze just right. Cleanest air I'd had in my lungs since last time I was here. Carmel is very small. You can drive from one end to the other in five minutes, any direction. The village's southern boundary is Santa Lucia Street, but there's no sign there to tell you that. The old Mission where Father Junipero Serra's bones are buried is in the city only by a sort of jiggering of the boundary line. Go north or east and you know you're out of town when numbers begin to appear on the houses. There are no addresses in Carmel. You have to say something like "third house north of Twelfth on the east side of Lincoln" to let people know where you are. You get your mail by hiking to the post office. I've often thought that hike up and down the hills is what keeps the old people spry.

The western edge of town is, of course, the Pacific Ocean, or that little scoop of it the maps call Carmel Bay. The wide margin of beach has the whitest sand and the coldest water on the central California coast.

I drove up Sixth Avenue to my new residence and pulled in under a cypress tree out of the traffic. Too late in the day to do any snooping. Too tired, anyhow. Too early to go to bed. It dawned on me that I hadn't eaten since breakfast. The files had arrived and Reiko and I had been busy straightening them up and she had been making innumerable cups of tea on a hot plate that materialized out of nowhere.

Making a decision about where to eat on this chunk of land bounded on three sides by elements of the Pacific is not easy. There are more than three hundred restaurants here, maybe fifty of 'em pretty good. And they change so often, you're always taking a chance. I said the hell with it and drove down to the Old Ranch, a quaint collection of buildings that sits behind the Mission. They have a pretty decent restaurant and a few cottages and the Barn, where, on certain nights, there is loud music. I used to stay there until they duded up the rooms and priced them out of my class. But it's got the location and the view. A very small house with this kind of view (along with termites and dry rot) would cost upwards of $400,000.

Marie was in the bar when I arrived, and she greeted me with a big gravel-voiced hello. She runs the motel operation during the odd hours, and she and I go back quite a few years. "Riordan, you old bastard! What's going on with the upper crust that brings you here?"

"I'm here permanently, honey. One of my satisfied customers who can't stay out of trouble is financing my move to Monterey and I'm living in a house he owns on the hill, up at Sixth and Santa Rita. He's a jealous husband, Marie, multiplied by about six. An old client with a history of paranoia, stupidity, and matrimony. But I'm tickled to be here. How are you?"

"Late nights and early mornings, Riordan. Sundays and holidays. The hard jobs, the dumb jobs."

We talked of times past and how the world was going to hell and what was happening to all the fine old things of Carmel. But I was hungry and made an excuse to go into the dining room.

"Come see me tomorrow, Riordan. I'm always here at six a.m."

The steak was pretty good, but close to overdone. I don't like it just seared on both sides and bloody in the middle. But I don't like it gray either. I was tired. And the sun had gone down. I drove home, watched a M*A*S*H rerun on some local independent, dozed through whatever came after it, and let the sound of the silence of the Carmel night put me to sleep.

3

She pushed the door open very slowly and sent me inside with her eyes.

I WAS IN this small room with no windows and the sound of battle in the distance. Then there was a knocking at the door. They've found me, I thought, although I had no idea who the hell had found me. I was terrified, though, and looked for a place to hide as the knocking stopped. Then I woke up.

"Hold it, hold it!" I tried to clear the fog out of my head. In a second, I knew where I was and what the sound was: somebody was banging the bejesus out of the rusty knocker on the front door and shouting at the same time.

I crawled out of bed and opened the window. "Who is it?"

"It's me, Riordan, Marie. Open up!" No question. That voice is unmistakable.

My first reaction was pure anger. "What the hell do you want?"

"Riordan, let me in. I need your help."

Now, Marie usually has a "well, screw you" sound to her gravelly voice. Some of that was still there, but mixed with a kind of urgency that compelled me to jump out of bed and put on my pants. I ran down the narrow staircase and across the cold floor tiles in my bare feet.

When I opened the door, Marie's expression was one I'd never seen before. Usually so in charge, so contained, she looked shaken and scared, her face drawn and gray.

"Thanks, Riordan," she said softly. "Now, put something on your feet and get in the truck."

Without thinking to question her, I dashed back up the stairs, pulled on a T-shirt and slid into my sandals. Then, like an obedient ten-year-old, I ran down the stairs and got in the truck. The lady had said to get in the truck.

"What's it all about?"

She stared straight ahead as we plunged down Sixth Avenue at forty miles an hour and swung left onto Junipero, ignoring the brake pedal.

"Where are we going?"

"You'll see."

I looked at my watch for the first time that morning. Quarter to seven.

Marie ignored all traffic signs and maintained speed until she hung a right at the Mission and headed for the Old Ranch. If a Carmel Police patrol car was anywhere around, we missed it. Too bad. They need a little excitement now and then. But we were out of their jurisdiction now.

"Why me?" I asked.

"Shut up!"

The tires squealed in protest as we turned into the Ranch property. We took an immediate hard left down the road by the tennis courts. Half a dozen of the Ranch's cottages are strung along by the courts and we pulled up in front of the next to last in the row.

Marie switched off the ignition and turned to me. She was tense again. She nodded at the cottage, the door of which was ajar.

Marie's voice was an almost inaudible rasp. "Woman named Lord. Sheila Lord. Been living here for the last year and a half. You remember when the new people came in and we booted out all the old long-termers and cleaned up these places. Well, business wasn't so good the last couple of winters, what with those goddam storms. So when she came in, we made her a rate and she paid her rent. Single woman, sort of an artist, paying twelve hundred a month for a dinky cottage."

Marie was loosening up now, breathing a bit more easily. "I don't know where she got the money, Riordan, and I don't give a damn.

Some kind of rich crazy, maybe. But she was a little slow this month. I stopped by yesterday and she was falling all over herself apologizing. But she told me that if I'd come back this morning on my way to the office, she'd have the cash. Well, I came by, and...." Her voice trailed off.

"Get out, Riordan."

I obeyed.

She nodded me ahead of her as we approached the open door. The July fog was beginning to burn off, but there was no light in the cottage.

She pushed the door open very slowly and sent me inside with her eyes.

I stood in a tiny living room. The shades were down and the light was dim. And all that I immediately noticed was the dust swirling in a shaft of light from the open door.

Within seconds, though, I was able to see the nude body of a woman in the semi-darkness. The head and torso lay on a chaise longue directly opposite the door, with the legs trailing gracefully onto the floor.

My eyes were drawn, however, to a sheet of drying blood from a ragged wound in her throat. The wide red stain ran between and around her full breasts and aslant across her lower ribs to the navel.

"Sheila Lord. Pretty good artist, some say. I sure as hell don't know."

Marie's voice and demeanor had returned to normal, as if sharing this ghastly sight with me had relieved her burden. She was almost her crusty old self again.

I tore my gaze away from the body on the couch and checked the room with what I hoped was a professional eye. Not actually any sign of a struggle. Sloppy housekeeping, maybe, but no fight. It was probably always like this. Bookshelves—all around the room—bookshelves loaded randomly with books and papers and junk. A layer of dust on everything.

"Have you called the sheriff?"

"Christ, no, Riordan. Only thing I could think of was to get you. Hell, you're some kind of a cop, aren't you?"

"Marie," I said, slowly and deliberately, "what we have here is a murder. There's no question. Somebody has killed this woman by jamming a sharp instrument into her throat. Go up to the office and call the sheriff. Quickly. The sooner they get people out here, the better."

I was convinced that a woman who was suicide-prone would not strip, arrange herself on a chaise longue like a Rubens painting, and then punch a hole in her jugular with some sort of lethal instrument.

Marie left me in the dark room standing in a patch of foggy bright light, looking at a naked corpse with blood-covered breasts and bony knees.

As I watched, the body began to move. I think I made some sort of noise as it slid slowly to the floor, the arms and legs in impossible positions. A slender easel in the corner was dislodged by the impact and toppled into the center of the room. The painting it had held fell squarely into the lighted area at my feet.

I have been involved in a few murder cases, more or less incidentally. A woman scorned threatens to geld her erstwhile lover with a snub-nosed revolver and aims too high. An insurance "accident" turns out to have been neatly arranged. But never before had I experienced the shock of seeing the victim of such an artistic murder, posed in a certain way, revealed by the swinging of a door. It was almost too theatrical.

I looked down at the painting. It was after seven o'clock and beginning to get lighter. What fog there had been was burning off quickly.

I know a little something about art. Helen and I started painting together years ago. She was very good, with an instinct for color and form. I just painted dogs. Somehow or other, no matter what I wanted to paint, it came out a dog. I don't mean that it was bad. It was a dog—an Irish setter, a poodle, a Yorkie. My dogs are mostly stored away, but I do have a number of good original oils, mostly by Carmel artists.

The painting on the floor of the cottage was oil on canvas, about 20 by 24 inches. Conventional. Ordinary size and shape. What blew my mind was that the painting depicted in strong, bold colors and strokes the scene that had stunned me only minutes before.

The nude female figure in the picture reclined on a chaise in a languorous pose, a slight smile on her face in contrast to the obscene red hole in her throat from which a wash of blood spread around and between her breasts. I bent down and touched the surface with a finger. It came away crimson, and I hastily wiped it on the bare wooden floor.

I decided to get the hell out of there. The sheriff would want things as they were. I had already witnessed a substantial change in the original scene. The body was now crumpled grotesquely on the floor, and the easel lay at right angles to the corpse with the top just touching the bloody midsection. And the painting lay almost squarely in the middle of that tiny, dusty room.

4

"Shit," said Deputy Holman, almost inaudibly.

I WALKED UP TO the Ranch office slowly, shivering in the cool of the morning. The chill ocean breeze knifed right through my rumpled chinos and cotton T-shirt.

Marie had the coffee on when I got into the office. An electric heater was just beginning to make the room comfortable. Marie was silent, stunned. She had called the sheriff's office on my instructions, and a crew was on its way.

"Didja close the door, Riordan?"

"Yes, and it locked. You've got the key?"

"Twenty of 'em. They lose 'em or wander off with 'em, y'know."

At that moment a plump young man with uncombed hair and photo-grey sunglasses came in to pay his bill. Across his too-tight magenta sweatshirt ran the legend, "Where the hell is Carmel-by-the-Sea?"

Well, I can tell you. It's on the underside—call it the southeast corner—of the stubby Monterey Peninsula which forms the bottom of Monterey Bay, curving down from Santa Cruz on the central coast of California. It has about five thousand permanent and semi-permanent residents and is 130 miles south of San Francisco and 350 miles north of Los Angeles. On any given summer Sunday, when the sun overcomes the fog, the number of people lying on the beach and wandering up and down Ocean Avenue is staggering. I suspect it approaches the population to the third power.

It is a lousy place for a murder.

I have this perfectly illogical conviction that murder shouldn't happen in nice places. But it does. People kill people without regard for the climate or the beauty of the scenery. That bothers me. The Ranch is a totally inappropriate place for a murder scene. It's so bucolic, so tranquil. Just a bunch of old buildings, only recently spruced up and painted, that used to be the nucleus of a dairy farm operated by the friars who ran the Mission San Carlos Borromeo de Carmelo a few hundred yards away.

I've just become a Carmel resident, but I strongly suspect that I will never become a member of the club. Some of us will always be in a kind of limbo: we're not tourists—but we're not the anointed, either. There are families with old money and families with new money. The newer they are, the more money they need. There are movie stars and TV personalities. There's the business crowd—proprietors of shops and restaurants—and there are the old grass-rooters who don't have much money but whose families have been here forever.

Then there are the artists and the writers and the musicians. The story goes that the whole art colony thing began after the San Francisco quake of 1906. Many artists, writers, and musicians were left homeless by the big shake (I suspect a lot of 'em were homeless anyhow) and decided to settle in Carmel. The town now has an impossible number of art galleries. You can't always read what the writers write or hear what the musicians compose. But you can sure see a lot of inferior seascapes.

I think the only way I'm ever going to get famous is to develop a few seascapes and maybe a couple of pastorals, and paint 'em over and over again for the tourists. Well, maybe I won't get famous. Just rich, which is even better.

But there's a lot of real art here, too. What was it Marie said about Sheila Lord? "Pretty good artist, some say."

A white sheriff's cruiser with a big green stripe on either side rolled up outside with two uniforms and a civilian inside. Through the office window I could see a white van moving through the ranch gate. The fog was nearly all burned off now, and just a wisp or two would occasionally drift by.

It was Tuesday morning. Very little happens on Tuesdays.

Important restaurants are closed. Tuesday lacks the vicious bite of Monday and the glowing promise of Friday.

The young uniformed officers walked into the room looking very serious. I can't imagine what they thought of me, sitting there unshaven, in rumpled pants and T-shirt, slightly blue bare feet in sandals.

The tall, sandy-haired one spoke. "My name is Holman. This is Deputy Hernandez. One of you called about a dead body? Possible murder victim?"

He looked at Marie and then at me. I suppose on the phone Marie's voice is as deep as mine. But this guy was probably not the one who answered the call.

Marie spoke up. "I called. This is Riordan. He's a private cop. He'll take you down and show her to you."

Holman looked at me dubiously.

"The deceased is a woman? You sure she's dead?"

Maybe I should have taken her pulse. But with most of her blood spilled all over her and the rest on the floor, I didn't think of it. "She's dead, Deputy. No doubt."

Marie wouldn't look me in the eye as she pressed the key to the cottage into my hand, walked quickly to her chair, sat down and stared at her desk.

On the way to Sheila Lord's cottage we had to pass under a cluster of three old eucalyptus trees. They put out a pleasant scent and a lot of hard little pods that crunch underfoot. They also drip a gum that hardens quickly on automobiles and forms a permanent part of the finish. I remembered irrelevantly that I had won a school spelling bee once on the word "eucalyptus," when I didn't know what one was.

Those deputies looked like little kids to me. It bothers me that cops and baseball players all look like little kids. Especially baseball players. They ought to be big guys with baggy pants and tobacco juice on their shirts. I suspected that neither of these young officers had been involved in a murder investigation before. It turned out I was right.

I watched their faces when we unlocked the door and they got their first look at the body. I guess they'd seen the results of some nasty car accidents: people torn and twisted in sudden death. But this was different. The stark contrast of the darkening blood against that ivory body was something out of a Vincent Price movie shot in cheap color.

The civilian who arrived with Holman and Hernandez had not been introduced. It really wasn't necessary. He carried an old Speed Graphic and a camera bag, and his job was to take pictures.

The white van had rolled quietly behind us as we walked to the cottage. I knew it contained a medical examiner and a couple of attendants from the coroner's office.

We stood looking at the bloody body on the floor for at least a full minute.

"Shit," said Deputy Holman, almost inaudibly. Hernandez looked a little ill.

The photographer, a young man with long hair and a straggly beard, was not quite as sensitive as the two officers, and he began his picture-taking routine with an air of boredom.

Holman composed himself. He became all business. "You find the body, sir?"

"No. The lady at the office saw it first. She came after me. I've got a little house uptown. I was here when the body hit the floor, though. It had been kind of sprawled on the chaise longue—and just slid down in a heap. That was when the easel fell."

"Did you see a—weapon, sir?"

Only at that moment did it occur to me that I had not seen a knife or anything else that might have made the puncture wound in the woman's throat. Hadn't even thought to look.

"No, as a matter of fact."

"We'd better look then. Mr. Riordan, you can help if you like. But don't touch the body...or anything. The sergeant will want it left as is."

Homicides in Monterey County outside of city limits are investigated by a sergeant's team from the sheriff's office. The head man of this group was no doubt on his way.

The two deputies and I, shoulder to shoulder, just about spanned the room. We moved slowly together, peering intently at the floor like a company of infantry policing up the area.

As we moved gingerly around the corpse, examining all the shaded corners, I could hear the ping of tennis balls being hit fifty feet away on the nearest court. There was no crowd of curious spectators outside. The sheriff's car was parked up at the office; only the white van was parked near the cottage. There had been no tennis players when we came down the road, and the people in the other cottages had either got out early or were still asleep.

There was no sharp instrument lying around the living room, at least that we could find. It was not an impressive room, except for the bookshelves on three walls. Two small upholstered chairs to our right flanked a round drum table which supported a tall lamp of plain design.

The easel had been standing in the right front corner, concealed from me originally behind the swing of the door. The floor was a good grade of bare pine, wide boards laid a long time ago. A couple of well-worn throw rugs lay in the traffic path. The body covered a corner of a fairly handsome Oriental that must have cost a few bucks. Hernandez opened the drapes over the window on the north wall. Two smaller windows on either side of the front door were thinly covered by faded curtains.

We moved into the bedroom. A double bed, mussed, with the covers thrown back, a small table with a reading lamp and a stack of magazines, a chest of drawers and a closet full of fairly expensive clothes. The small bathroom had a stall shower, a basin, and a john—and enough room to turn around in if you were careful.

The kitchen was a surprise. Small and efficient. None of the vague sloppiness of the living room and the bedroom. Everything in its place and spotlessly clean. A red-and-white checked tablecloth covered a small table into which were nestled three wooden chairs. The cabinets were filled with cans and boxes and bottles, neatly arranged.

A nice little place for a single lady artist, you know? But it sure as hell didn't tell us much about the person who lived—and died— here.

"Hello in there. Oh, Jesus, this is beautiful!" The voice came from the front door. The medical examiner had poked his head in. The two deputies and I trooped back into the living room.

He was a short dark man in a short-sleeved tan shirt and khaki pants. He carried a doctor's black bag which he set on the floor as he knelt to take a close look at the body. He assumed a mock-pontifical air.

"Gentlemen, this is, in my hasty but humble professional opinion, a homicide. Somebody opened up a vein and this poor lady has bled herself dry, just about. Exsanguinated, as it were. Any weapon?"

"Haven't found anything yet, Doctor," said Holman.

The examiner thrust his face up close to the wound, his head tilted to engage the bottom half of his bifocals.

"Hard telling what made this. Could have been a kitchen knife. A dull one. Could even have been a pocket knife. Some kind of sharp instrument. Not too sharp, though. Pretty raggedy cut, more like a puncture with a deliberate twist. Killer knew where to put the hole, though...straight into the jugular."

He looked at us through thick lenses. "Could've got the carotid, too. Would have been quicker."

He gave us an ugly grin. "That's kosher, you know."

He opened his bag and tugged on a pair of surgical rubber gloves. Gently, he touched the wound, and studied it for a few seconds. He then began methodically to inspect the flesh and muscle tone, pressing his fingers into the body at various points and examining the reaction. Suddenly, he stood up.

"Not much I can do here, boys. You want to chalk the position, take some more pictures? I'm going to take her down to the morgue. Ought to do an autopsy as soon as possible. I'm curious about this lady. Something pretty strange about the way she died."

He was examining the woman's hands and arms. "My people are outside. Tell 'em to come in."

I watched as the men from the coroner's office handled the dead woman with surprising respect and tenderness. Gently they straightened out the limbs which had stiffened in awkward positions. With great care, they slid the body into the usual plastic cocoon and lifted it onto a stretcher. In a few moments they were gone. About that time, the medical examiner seemed to discover me.

"Who the hell is this? The manager? Some kind of relative?"

"Sorry, Dr. Marshall, this is Mr. Riordan. He's a private investigator who happens to be a friend of the lady in the office. She went after him after she found the body."

Marshall peeled off his right glove and stuck out his hand. His small dark eyes narrowed, but there was a smile on his lips.

"Hey, I think I saw this on TV. The private eye just happens to be near the scene of the crime. What's the story? You get much of this kind of business?"

I mumbled something about just trying to help out a friend, and found myself embarrassed and tongue-tied. Fortunately, Marshall lost interest in me very quickly, and departed briskly to accompany the body to the morgue.

5

"The lady was disenchanted, Pat."

Good old George, who was responsible for my being here in the first place, had given me the names of some drinking holes his wife seemed to favor. I had promised him that I would make discreet inquiries. It was a job I'd done before, beginning with wife number two (or was it three?), and I didn't relish the prospect.

I have no idea how much money George Spelvin has. I am not really in communication with his kind of wealth. Many of the people who employ me are of George's caste; few, if any, have ever struggled with the problem of how to pay the rent or the electric bill.

One of my clients is a rather bland rich man who inherited his position as head of a prosperous manufacturing firm. He takes his position and good fortune for granted. His is old money, and lots of old San Francisco money means a mansion in Hillsborough, an enclave of the very rich south of the City. He suffers from a deep-rooted sense of security. He cannot understand why I expect him to pay his bills in a reasonable length of time. But he's smart enough to delegate authority and keep the money rolling in.

George, however, never pretended to be employed. Occasionally, he would drop a corporate name, most frequently that of a prominent conglomerate that had started out as a lumber mill. Once or twice in my company, he had mentioned one of the world's largest banks in a way that suggested he had a substantial piece of the action. And he seemed actually pleased when the phony oil shortage a few years back made gasoline prices go up.

His checks were always generous and always good. We had an arrangement: I would serve George in any capacity as long as it was legal, and he would pay me what he thought my services were worth. Things worked out just fine for me.

George gave many parties and, in the months after Helen's death, I had been invited to a few of them at his Tiburon condo. I never knew anybody, so I would usually stand near the bar and drink twelve-year-old Scotch until some of the social types would disappear. On the morning after one of George's parties, I would frequently awaken in my Russian Hill flat in bed with a lady whose name I could not remember. As often as not, I could not even recall her face. I had somehow made a conquest, driven back across the Golden Gate bridge, managed to consummate the union—and, alas, couldn't remember a thing about any of it.

My host, on the other hand, despite his prodigious intake of booze and his tendency to paranoia, never forgot anything.

"How the hell do you always manage to run off with the best-looking girl at the party?" he would ask, and proceed to describe my entire evening in detail, to my embarrassment.

But I like George very much. And I owe him a lot. So I had to get on with the investigation of his most recent marital folly.

I was pretty nervous about this Sheila Lord business. I don't shy from blood or violence. I was a combat soldier in Korea, barely eighteen, when a guy alongside me got half his face sliced off by a piece of shrapnel. But despite all my years of dealing with violent emotions and unstable people, despite my experience with sudden death, I was upset about Lord's murder.

When the medical examiner left and the young officers sent me home with the admonition to "hold yourself in readiness for questioning" (which simply means "don't leave town, buddy"), I prevailed on a silent Marie to drive me back.

It was pushing ten o'clock and I was hungry. I changed and walked downtown to a little restaurant for a couple of eggs over easy and about a gallon of black coffee. It was going to be a sunny day, the breeze was gentle and cool, and I walked around a while to get my head together.

OK, Riordan, you are here for a job. Sheila Lord doesn't have anything to do with you and you couldn't care less about Sheila Lord. That painting on the floor, though—the rosy, smiling nude, oil on canvas, 20 by 24—that bothered me. The style was familiar. The memory of the painting kept poking out of my subconscious and I kept shoving it back.

I called George about noon and caught him in the bar at the Lodge, as I knew I would. He already had about half a heat on, and I'm not sure he understood anything I said as I tried to describe the events of the morning.

As far back as anybody could remember, George had been hitting some kind of bar at about ten in the morning; from places like the Lodge, that put a fresh doily under every drink, to places like the 2 A.M. Club in Mill Valley, where you lay your money on the line and the bartenders pour right from the bottle without that intervening quarter-pound of glass called a jigger. George had an incredible capacity for booze and he bore a charmed life.

He really had no notion where his pretty wife spent her afternoons. She did not take tennis lessons, so there was no well-tanned tennis pro with bleached hair and a Tom Selleck mustache to divert her.

There was another problem: I had never seen this wife. George had produced a picture taken several years ago, but the woman in it might have been anybody's good-looking blonde. And her name was (rather appropriately, I thought) Debbie.

I was wearing a navy and white striped shirt, an eggshell jacket with knitted cuffs and collar, off-white tennis shoes, knee-length sweat socks and white tennis shorts. You could tell me from the tourists because the shorts fit. There is a golden tan that goes with this outfit that I just didn't have. You don't get a tan in San Francisco, even if you play tennis every day. But this is a native costume for middle-aged men with gray hair on the prowl in Carmel. And I always try to blend in with the surroundings. Besides, I'm a little vain about being without a paunch and having legs that are good enough to play one of the lesser nobles in *Richard III*.

But as soon as I started asking questions about Debbie Spelvin in my first bar, people started murmuring softly and examining me out of the corners of their eyes. Yes, some of them knew Debbie. Yes, she did come in once in a while—alone. Somebody else thought she lived with some guy in Pebble Beach. She never said much and she smiled a lot. Built like the proverbial brick outbuilding.

It was a fruitless, boring task. My mind wasn't on my work and my heart wasn't in it. A picture of a naked, bloody corpse was in my mind; a lady with a madonna face and auburn hair, whose expression was tranquil—even gently smiling—in violent death. An artist. An artist? Why were there no paintings on the walls? No art supplies? Only an unsteady easel with a painting on it, a painting of the dead lady herself?

As I have said, my experience with murder has been limited. I didn't serve time with the police force as many of my competitors did. I got to be a private investigator out of sheer desperation and the good offices of a kind and generous friend. After Korea, I went to law school on the GI Bill and managed to get a degree. At the time, I was engaged to a girl I had waited all my life for.

Just at bar exam time, my fiancée tearfully informed me that she had fallen in love with a successful young orthodontist and was terribly sorry she could not marry me. I nobly let her out with a kiss on the forehead worthy of Ronald Colman—and on the night before the bar exam, I went out and got thoroughly ripped. How I made it out of bed the next morning I do not know, but I took the bar exam and finished not quite dead last.

Some hazy weeks after that, when I was running out of money and staying drunk most of the time, Al Jennings took me in. Al was a kindly soul, and an old friend of my father. He claimed to have been a Pinkerton operative with Hammett, and at the time of my debacle was running an investigative service out of a little one-man office in the Flood Building.

When Al died suddenly of a heart attack a few years later, I was on my own. He had been a widower, childless, and the business passed on to me, lock, stock, and unpaid bills.

At any rate, I never was a cop. And, even though I had worked with the police on occasion during my investigative career, I really didn't think like one. At least, I *think* I didn't think like a cop.

I sat at the end of another bar and ordered another Perrier with lime. This stuff and coffee are all I drink these days since Reiko took charge of me. After Helen's death I made a serious attempt to drink all the scotch in San Francisco. It's what I call Irish suicide. Slow death—and you feel no pain.

A hand touched my shoulder and I turned to look into the handsome, bearded face of Greg Farrell.

"Pat, how are you?"

"Hello, Greg. A pleasure to meet a friend at this time of weariness and grief. Sit down. Have a glass of wine or something."

"What's the matter? You look healthy enough but you sure seem down."

"Did you know Sheila Lord?"

"Oh, yeah. I knew Sheila pretty well. I just heard what happened to her. It's in the *Herald*. Big headline on the front page."

"Did they mention my name?" I'm not a publicity hound, you understand, but everything helps.

"Hell, I never read the paper. Just the headlines you can see through that little window in the box. Poor Sheila. She was in one of my classes for a while. A really talented girl, Pat, but kind of flakey, y'know what I mean?"

I had known Greg for a lot of years. He was prominent in the Carmel art colony, a really extraordinary painter who managed to eke out a living selling a picture now and then and teaching in the Adult Education program. I have a couple of his things that are very good. There isn't enough wall space where I am now in George's little house to accommodate all the paintings I have.

A sudden thought hit me.

"Greg, if you had read the story in the paper, you'd know I was one of the first people on the scene this morning. Don't ask me why—it doesn't matter. But it struck me as pretty strange that Lord was first described to me as a painter, and yet there wasn't a piece of art in the place. Well, there was one—one painting on an easel stuck in a corner—but nothing on the walls."

The artist smiled as he slid onto the bar stool next to me.

"The lady was disenchanted, Pat. I don't know why, really. Maybe she just went dry. Anyhow, one Saturday night—I think it was in February—she took all of her paints, brushes, canvases, everything, out on the road in front of her house and set fire to the whole enchilada. On a Saturday night, mind you, when there was a big, loud wingding in high cog at the Barn and cars all over the place. And that stuff burns, Pat. All that turpentine, that oil. Well, the fire department was there in five minutes after somebody called and there just wasn't much to do. The whole mess went up with a whoosh! It was all over before anybody at the Barn knew about it."

"What had she been doing since the bonfire?" Sheila Lord's body loomed up in my mind again. It's a bad thing to see a murdered corpse. It gets a lot worse when you come to know the human being it used to be.

"Nobody knows, really." Greg was looking beyond me towards the Dutch door of the lounge. Its upper half was thrown open and the midsummer sun was still bright in the late afternoon.

"Nobody saw much of her after that, Pat. After the fire—and everybody in town knew about it—she just faded away. Oh, once in a while somebody would run into her down at Safeway. But that's it, as far as I know."

"How well...did you get to know her?"

"Well, like I said, she was a student. A good one...for a while."

"That's all? She was a pretty woman."

"She was that. I was attracted to her. You know me, Pat. Maybe I bought her coffee a few times. But why the quiz?"

"I don't know. Can't get her out of my mind. Sorry, Greg. Guess I came on like a detective. Let's change the subject. Are you teaching this summer?"

"Yeah, one class in oils, one drawing class. Enough to keep from starving."

"Good. Keep painting."

I got up to go. Too many things were going on in my mind. George should have a report this evening, but I really had nothing to report. I had another thought.

"Where did Lord come from, Greg? And how old was she?"

"San Jose, I think. Twenty-seven, twenty-eight, twenty-nine. I don't know."

"Can I get hold of you tomorrow?"

"Sure, Pat. At Sunset Center until noon or so. Down at the house in the afternoon. You've got the number, right?"

"Right. See you."

I watched him leave the bar. In a few minutes I paid my tab, overtipped the bartender, and went out through the Dutch door.

Greg had seemed straightforward about Sheila Lord. But something was gnawing at me. I never knew him just to "buy coffee" for a woman who looked like Sheila Lord.

6

"She's no artist, goddammit, she slops paint on canvas."

WHEN HELEN AND I decided, on a whim, to take up painting, we looked around for a place to start. We were in Carmel on vacation. Maybe we were looking for new challenges. Maybe we just got tired of making conversation. Anyhow, we checked with Armand Colbert, an old friend, a man of many talents and an infallible source of information.

"Greg Farrell is teaching, I think. He's a friend and he's good." His voice took on an edge. "But you better know what you want. Norman Rockwell he's not. If you want representational, go elsewhere. If you want art, find Greg."

I called the Adult Ed office and was told that Greg taught in one of the buildings that make up Carmel's Sunset Center, an old school complex that has been converted into a gathering of the arts. On that particular day, however, he had his class outdoors in the parking lot of the River School, which had an impressive, unobstructed view of Point Lobos.

It was a chilly April afternoon when we drove down to see him. He stood among his students—mostly ladies of a certain age—like a sea captain, braced against the wind: pea-jacketed, knit capped, and bearded like a pirate.

There was a hint of mistrust in his eyes when I introduced myself. The conversation was brief. I had a satisfactory opening ploy: we had bought one of his paintings, a great good humored, splashy still life which brightened up our kitchen.

Greg warmed up a bit and we got around to arranging some lessons, in class and private. Helen blossomed right away. She might have become known for the wonderful impressionistic paintings she produced from the start. My first efforts would have made it in the third grade.

It got so that every time we came to Carmel—five or six times a year, a month in the summer—we'd get together with Greg, join whatever class he was teaching, have lunch, visit his studio down the coast. We became friends.

Greg is a very private person. For years we made good conversation and laughed at each other's jokes. We were both movie buffs and could talk for hours about pictures we had seen.

But some things he never spoke of, things that still caused him pain, I guess. Now and then there would be a vague reference to a marriage that apparently had ended badly. And once in a while the Viet Nam war would creep in and then swiftly out of our conversation.

He would proclaim that in his early youth, he had wanted to grow up to be either a pirate or a cowboy.

"You know my basic philosophy, don't you? 'What would John Wayne do?'" He spoke this profundity with a straight face, but with a devilish twinkle in his eye.

Greg would sprawl on a couch in his faded denim shirt and ragged levis, boots up to his knees, and philosophize:

"The only assets I have are a good head of hair and the ability to drive fast backwards," he would say seriously.

At other times (and I tend to agree with this):

"Just about every conversation can be reduced to this: One guy says, 'We're all going to hell in a handbasket!' The other guy says, 'Ain't life grand!' Maybe we all ought to carry little signs around, one in the right-hand pocket and the other in the left, with those two sentiments on 'em. Instead of wasting a lot of words, a person could just hold up one sign or the other, according to how he feels."

The bright light of the summer afternoon made me squint as I emerged from the shadowy bar into Ocean Avenue. Turning right up the hill, I started towards the pay phone at the corner of Lincoln by the library. On the way, I searched my mind for something to say to George. I was still thinking when I punched out the numbers.

His voice was sharp as he came on the line. Sober?

"Hello, George, this is Riordan."

"What do you know, Pat?" His voice dropped to a whisper. "Please don't try to spare me." He *was* sober.

"Not a damn thing, my friend. I have checked out the bars you mentioned, and there's no evidence that she ever did anything but have a friendly drink. I don't have any notion where she is."

"I know where she is, Riordan. She came home about a half hour ago and went right up to her studio without saying hello. How she can stay up there, I don't know. The place stinks of paint and turpentine."

Something clicked in my head. "She's an artist, George? You didn't mention that."

"She's no artist, goddammit, she slops paint on canvas. Hell, Riordan, she's only been painting a year or so. Still taking lessons. And they don't seem to be doing her any good."

"Where is she studying? That might give me a lead."

"Cheap course. Adult Education at the Sunset Center. You know the guy. One of those Big Sur hippies. Greg Farrell."

I told him I'd report back and hung up. I pictured the aristocratic Spelvin: the tightly curled gray hair, the gold scarab at the throat, the expensive shirt open to the sternum, tucked into the narrow pants. Nobody ever looked more like a retired Wimbledon champion. But George had never touched a racquet in his life, trained on Dewar's, and would probably outlive all of his tennis-playing friends.

I have to admit that I was a little shocked to learn that one of George Spelvin's wives was an art student, and angry at myself for not mentioning her name to Greg in the bar. It amused me, however, to hear George refer to Farrell as a "Big Sur hippie." Greg could certainly pass for what Pebble Beach folks thought of as a hippie. He has longish hair and that full dark beard, and he never wears anything but the faded denim shirts and jeans and knee-length boots. A hippie he is not, though, by a long shot. And the canyon where he lives is only halfway to Big Sur.

I was standing at the phone, one of those open-air jobs Superman could never change clothes in, where the phone books are always damp. A thin lady in a severely tailored gray tweed suit was noisily clearing her throat behind me. I begged her forgiveness and got out of the way.

It wasn't dinner time yet. The car was parked down on San Carlos where there were no time limits. Carmel has a squad of painfully conscientious young women who run around town in three-wheeled bugs called Cushmans and make chalk marks on left rear tires. If your car is still there on the next round, they write you a little seven dollar note. It is a source of pride to me that in the almost thirty years I have been coming to this town, I have never gotten a ticket. So I park where the bike and chalk ladies don't go. If I do have to venture into their territory, I always have one eye on my watch.

I crossed Ocean and started up the hill towards Dolores. My mind was churning with the various bizarre occurrences of the day. I had two female unknowns that might link up into some kind of equation. One was dead, and the other one I hadn't laid eyes on yet.

The tourists were beginning to thin out, and I walked slowly up the hill, idly window-shopping, almost as if I were trying to avoid thinking about the case at hand—*cases* at hand. Does anybody ever buy these expensive, good-looking clothes in the shop windows? Not in the summertime, surely. Summertime tourists are clutching ice-cream cones or chocolate chip cookies and pushing prams and dragging fat kids. My God, that couple over there, bulging in their jeans, with their arms around each other, look exactly like Tenniel's drawing of Tweedle-Dum and Tweedle-Dee.

So much changes so often and so suddenly. Shops and restaurants are here one trip and gone the next. They seem to be transformed overnight. I don't like to seem sentimental—it's not good for the image—but I get a little sad when I see one of these tiny shops fold. Very often it is the end of life's golden dream for those people. All the bucks squirreled away over the years for that "little shop in Carmel"—all of it down the toilet.

I walked around the corner onto Dolores. There was a smell of wood smoke in the air. The smell of wood smoke is always in the air here, summer or winter. As I walked down toward Seventh, I was aware of some things old and some things new. Across the street that wonderful little English country cottage, another of Hugh Comstock's rustic fairy-tale designs, which daily attracts long lines of patient customers craving tea and scones and buttered toast. To my right, the first stages of a tiny park, healing an ugly vacant lot that had been there for years while the city council waged a petty and seemingly interminable battle over what should be done with it.

I had nearly reached the end of the block when I passed the restaurant I have always called Armand's place, even though it was really a Colbert family enterprise and isn't even theirs any more. I had known Armand first as an artist. I have a couple of his paintings from a period I call the "early and only." He was never content with just painting. He and his brother had started as musicians, writing and recording film scores and commercials in L.A. Armand was the first of the family to come to Carmel and he quickly made himself a part of the scene. He set up a photography studio, and peddled his leathercraft work through local department stores and later through a shop of his own. He got a popular sandal franchise and built it into a thriving business. Everything made money. He told me once that he had designed women's clothes and had run a couple of dress shops in Riverside when he was about twenty. I believe it.

A few years ago, the family bought a little rundown house up the hill and turned it into a restaurant. Now you might think, on the face of it, that another restaurant is what Carmel needs like it needs another art gallery. But now it is one of the two or three most popular eating places in town. They call it Casablanca.

Armand! It dawned on me that if I was ever to get a handle on the complicated situation that had been presented to me, Armand could give me some perspective. I couldn't get Sheila Lord out of my mind. I did not doubt that Armand knew the murdered woman. He knows everybody—and everybody's business. He and Greg are old friends—and Greg had a personal tie to Miss Lord as well as a current acquaintance with Debbie, the wandering wife of my client.

I made a mental note to see Armand in the morning and closed my mind for the day. I drove back to my cottage, took a quick shower, and then wandered down to the Adobe Inn for some barbecued ribs. The latest Clint Eastwood movie was playing at the Golden Bough, and I wanted to see it. Clint, whose pictures play Carmel for months sometimes, is a local resident part-time and an astute businessman full-time, who had the foresight to buy up a lot of well-located property here and out in the Carmel Valley back in the days when it was almost reasonable. I was pleased with the movie, a sort of New Wave western, when Clint neatly disposed of eleven bad guys in the last four minutes.

Then home to bed like Pepys, to write my journal in my mind. Sleep is a fugitive after that kind of day.

It was cool, and the fog was rolling in. The surf thumped in the distance and a breeze whistled outside my bedroom window as I lay playing the past fourteen hours on the wide screen in my brain. The last time I looked at my watch it was two a.m., and I can't remember what I was thinking about when I finally drifted off.

7

"Would you kindly tell me now, Mr. Riordan, what you did and what you saw yesterday morning?"

I WAS UP, brushing my teeth and thinking about breakfast, when somebody knocked on the door. I walked down the stairs and opened the door with my mouth full of white foam.

"Mr. Riordan, I'm Detective Sergeant Balestreri, Sheriff's Department. Like to talk to you."

The sergeant's face was expressionless and his voice was a monotone. I had a quick flash of Jack Webb and Harry Morgan in the last *Dragnet* series. Indicating my muteness by pointing to the toothbrush protruding from my mouth, I nodded to the officer to enter and went back up to the bathroom to spit and rinse.

When I returned, the sergeant was sitting in one of the armchairs, knees crossed, right foot waggling with just the hint of impatience.

"Yes, sir," I said, sitting on the couch. I waited, expectantly.

Balestreri looked tall, even sitting down. He was hatless and wore a down vest. His shock of dark hair was shot with gray. He wore a well-trimmed military mustache, and his eyebrows grew together across the bridge of his nose. Forty-one or -two, I'd guess, with the direct, clear look of one who had seen almost everything.

He drew a deep breath. "Missed you yesterday, Mr. Riordan. I got to the crime scene just a bit after you left. Holman and

45

Hernandez told me you're a PI. Would you kindly tell me now, Mr. Riordan, what you did and what you saw yesterday morning? From the time Mrs. Adams came after you until the people from my department arrived."

Frowning and closing my eyes, I tried to recite a moment-by-moment account of the period in question. Did a rather good job of it, too, sailing right through my adventures with the deputies and my brief exchange with the medical examiner.

Balestreri looked at me and said nothing for about a minute and a half. He studied a small notebook.

"It checks. What bothered me in the beginning was your story about the body falling off that couch so long after death. Medical people say it can happen, though. Something internal happens— makes the weight shift. I buy it."

The man didn't blink, I thought. Not once. Still hadn't. He had the most unblinking look I'd ever seen. I remembered a couple of confrontations I had with a former San Francisco police chief who, in addition to not blinking, never smiled and wore a bad toupee.

"I understand you're on friendly terms with an artist named Greg Farrell. Right?"

That was a shocker. I tried not to let the surprise show in my eyes. "Sure, I've known Greg a long time. Saw him yesterday afternoon, in fact. What's that got to do with...."

Balestreri smiled. "Mr. Riordan, you are pretty well known around here. Reasonably well thought of, I might add. I had to check you out. San Francisco police give you a clean bill of health. Carmel police have a record of a minor skirmish in a bar some years back. You paid the guy's dentist, and he was too ashamed to press charges. Nothing critical. Bartender I know says he served you and Farrell about five-fifteen yesterday."

A minor skirmish in a bar. Just after Helen died. There were many of those. The San Francisco ones didn't go on the record. I paid for the damage, if any, and my own hospital bills. But some of these small, senseless altercations are on the record in San Rafael, Mill Valley and, if I'm not mistaken, San Jose. I'd forgotten about Carmel. I'm usually so peaceful in Carmel.

"You want to know what the hell difference it makes whether or not you know Farrell. Well, the medical examiner is a very curious man. He couldn't wait to do an autopsy on Sheila Lord. Something about the fact that she had a hole in her throat that had to come from an instrument that wasn't too sharp—and yet showed no bruises or abrasions or other signs of struggle. And she bled to death from the jugular—which usually takes a while. She couldn't have done the job herself. There was no instrument. It wasn't done in another room, either. No sign of blood anywhere but on and around the body. And she died with a peaceful smile on her face, almost as though she was happy about it. So Marshall did a complete job on the body yesterday afternoon. You want to know what he found?"

For a sophisticated big city detective, I was beginning to feel like Linus without his blanket. Bogart would have lit a cigarette at this point. But I quit smoking fifteen years ago.

"Sergeant Balestreri," I said, as indignantly as I could, "you are baiting me. Kindly get to the point."

The man from the sheriff's office drew a long breath and leaned back in the chair, his hands on his knees.

"The lady was loaded with heroin, Riordan. Not enough to kill her. But far too much for a casual chipper. She wasn't an addict. A rank amateur. One pop in the crease of her left elbow. No scars, no other holes."

He sat erect, leaned towards me, and waved his little notebook in my face.

"We couldn't find any dope or user's equipment anywhere around, so we figure the murderer brought it in and took it away. Doc didn't find any evidence of rape. But—and this is sure pretty interesting, Riordan—she was two months pregnant. My sources in town tell me that it was probably Farrell's child. What do you say to that?"

8

"Why that name? Of all people!"

N OBODY NEEDS drugs here. Do you understand me? There is no drug problem in Carmel. Oh, well, once in a while a kid gets in trouble. A little pot, a little coke. A lot of kids have too much money and have never learned how to cure boredom with anything but chemistry. But nobody needs drugs!"

That kind of oversimplification wouldn't reach me ordinarily. But Armand Colbert was doing the talking, and I was doing the listening and wondering just how much to believe. Armand is seldom in doubt. He is a man of positive convictions, and he's usually right. Armand is not tall, nor is he physically overpowering. But he is smoothly handsome ("devastatingly attractive" Helen used to say), and a real presence in Carmel, with his faint accent and easy smile.

But the lady I had seen dead with blood all over her chest had been full of dope—hard stuff. Where there is hard stuff, there is trouble. Sheila Lord had been injected with enough of it to put her in a stupor. Shortly thereafter, somebody had opened her throat with a semi-sharp instrument. She died painlessly and didn't even know she was dying.

Balestreri's information about Greg Farrell's being the likely father of Lord's child was not particularly shattering to me. It did bother me that Greg had lied about his relationship with the woman. I wanted to talk to him. But my schedule called for a conference with Armand Colbert. Armand would be a fountain of information. He always is.

I was sitting with him in a cramped office over his restaurant. He, like everybody else in the village, had heard about the murder. But when I brought him the other disturbing facts in the case, he professed to be dumfounded.

Armand was on his feet, looking out a window into Fifth Avenue. His voice was subdued. "I remember when Sheila came to town. She was twenty-three, modestly pretty, and thrilled to be here. I gave her a job at the leather goods shop. She moved over to my sandal store later on. She loved just being here—leaving her little room every morning and walking to work in the fog. Doing the galleries. Going to concerts. By the way, you know the Bach Festival is on now, don't you? Sheila used to love the Bach Festival."

He paused. He had returned to the present only momentarily and had never looked at me. "She had a couple of affairs before she met Greg. Never lived with anybody. I don't think she really wanted to be an artist, although she had a lot of raw talent."

At the mention of Farrell, I stopped him. "Armand, are you telling me that Sheila Lord had a love affair with Greg?"

At last, he looked at me. "I really don't know. Greg and I haven't been close the last few years. No problem. I think it's just that I'm not really into painting anymore—and Greg is all artist."

Armand stroked his mustache. He closed his eyes for an instant, then opened them wide.

"How much do you know about Greg?"

The question took me by surprise. I had known Greg for nearly fifteen years. "Enough, I guess. Hell of an artist. He's never had the recognition he's deserved. Very bright guy. Great story teller. Lots of laughs."

I stopped. That was it. Pretty thin.

Armand sighed. "What you have seen is surface. Like some people see a painting. A flat plane on which colors are laid to represent something...or nothing. There is not good art and bad art. There is only art and non-art. The test of art—or one's appreciation for art—is the extent to which the observer feels the presence of the artist."

He stood up and began to pace back and forth in a narrow arc. "You've painted. You've been among painters. Take a walk around town. Look at the things in the gallery windows. Here's a seascape, there's a landscape, over there's a still life. All of them technically well executed. But one will stop you cold. You may walk on a few steps, but you'll turn back. And it won't be the colors or the technique or the lighting—or, for God's sake, the frame. It'll be the presence of the artist. If anybody who paints tells you he just wants his work appreciated and is indifferent about his presence, he's a goddam liar."

He sat down abruptly and struck the table with his fist. "Greg is a very complicated man. He seems cool—even irresponsible at times. But there is the steel of discipline in him. And you know where he got it? Annapolis. The Naval Academy."

I had heard some vague references to Farrell's military career. He had mentioned Viet Nam in my company. But I was hard-pressed to imagine him in a service academy.

"He came out of Annapolis and took a commission in the Army. Didn't know they could do that, did you? Well, he did and was one of the first officers in combat in Viet Nam. Went back for a second tour. Got shot up three times."

Armand assumed a matter-of-fact tone. Relating Greg's personal history seemed to relax him. He rocked back in his chair, tilting against the wall, his hands clasped behind his head.

"What about it, Pat. Think he could kill somebody?"

These revelations about the smiling, easy-going man I had known so long kept me silent for what seemed at least a full minute while Armand peered at me through half-closed eyes.

He picked up his story: "Sheila Lord had an aunt or some kind of relative who lived—maybe still lives—in a big place out on the Point. I think it's near Tor House, the Robinson Jeffers place. She'd go there once in a while, but the relationship was not all that happy. It was the relative who suggested that she move into the cottage at the Ranch. Maybe paid her rent. I know she quit her job after she started painting, and she didn't sell that much art."

"She wasn't working for you at that time?"

"No. I think she was waitressing or hostessing at the Adobe Inn."

"You don't know the relative's name?"

He shrugged: "I don't. Hard for you to believe, eh?"

It was. Armand knew *everything*.

"Who might know?"

"Greg might. I don't know."

I had bought a cheap notebook at the variety store and was jotting down small, significant items like your natural-born cinema or video detective. I wrote: "Greg might know Lord rel."

You may think that I had forsaken my mission on behalf of George Spelvin, and you'd be almost right. Debbie was in and out of my thoughts, although at this point she was more a concept than an image. She popped in just at that moment, so I seized the opportunity to ask: "Armand, this is sort of off the subject, but have you ever heard of a pretty lady named Debbie Spelvin?" I used the real family name, of course.

His brows went up and his mouth dropped open as he looked at me in disbelief. "Why that name? Of all people! Why do you bring up that one?" He was agitated. "If you really want to know about Greg Farrell's love life, *cherchez* cette *femme*! She's got a rich husband over in Pebble Beach, but it's all over town that she's madly in love with Greg." Armand looked genuinely angry. His head jerked as he spat out his words.

"Whoops, sorry," I said. "And by the way, from what you've told me, I'm sure Greg could have killed somebody in his war. But not Sheila Lord, Armand, not Sheila."

9

"Who is that insolent person?"

ADELE BLANCHARD has blue-white hair, a pallid complexion, and the air of a Prussian general. She has had tucks to rein in her wattles, and she wears tailored suits and sensible shoes. She wields a lot of influence in Carmel.

Like George Spelvin, Adele is old money, the source of which is lost in the fog of Pebble Beach, where Adele presently does not choose to live. Also like George, she has been a client of mine, although she would be reluctant to admit it.

Adele's only child Nancy has been a problem to her since puberty. Nancy was thoroughly spoiled before she could read, and had tried pot, booze, and sex by the time she was twelve. At sixteen, she ran off with the family's gardener, a muscular Latin of questionable character who was more than twice Nancy's age and the father of five. On George's recommendation, Adele hired me to bring her back.

It wasn't a difficult assignment. By the time I caught up with them, Nancy was thoroughly sick of Raul. She returned to her mother's home without a whimper. But she repeated the performance with a wide variety of men at least once a year until, at twenty-one, she was installed in a tiny cottage in the Carmel Woods, where the sun seldom intrudes and the neighbors never pry.

When I left Armand's place, I thought it might be a good idea to visit my office. So I drove over to Monterey in uncharacteristic sunshine to check into the new headquarters (as yet barren, sparsely furnished, and depressing) and receive the customary tongue-lashing from Reiko for staying away without phoning her for a couple of days.

She glared at me when I walked into the office. "It's a good thing I am a lady. I have every right to heap justifiable abuse on you, Riordan. I am this moment thinking of you in obscene, unspeakable anatomical terms. Why haven't you called me?"

We've played out this little scene before, many times. And she's always right. I bowed my head and apologized profusely. Then I carefully made my way past her desk to the inner office before she could cause me grievous bodily injury with a paperweight.

I sat down and contemplated an empty desk. No messages, no case files. I was settling back to do some serious thinking when the phone rang.

I could hear Reiko through the thin partition. Sometimes, just for the hell of it, she would answer the phone in Japanese.

"*Moshi-moshi,* Riordan's office."

A pause.

"Who am I? Well, who the hell are you?"

I picked up my phone in haste.

"Riordan here," I said in a very loud, authoritarian voice which was meant to get Reiko off the wire.

Adele Blanchard, who had never called me at my San Francisco office, came on in a flood of righteous indignation. "Mr. Riordan!" She always addressed me formally. "Who is that insolent person?" Her voice was unmistakable.

"I'm sorry, Mrs. Blanchard. My regular receptionist is ill...and you know how temporary help is." I lied with a big smile on my face.

That seemed to help. Her voice dropped a few decibels. "Mr. Riordan, what I have to discuss with you is very private. Can anyone...eavesdrop on our conversation?"

"One moment, Mrs. Blanchard."

I gently laid the phone on my desk and very quietly rose and opened the door into the reception area just in time to see Reiko silently replace her phone on its cradle. I glared at her as she had earlier glared at me, but she just waved a butterfly hand and turned to her IBM-PC.

"OK, Mrs. Blanchard. How may I help you?"

"It's Nancy, of course. She's gone again. I went up to her cottage this morning and it was pretty clear that she hadn't been there for several days. I've been nervous about her since that awful business with the Lord woman. They were friends, you know. Used to see a lot of each other before Sheila became such a recluse. As a matter of fact, I think Sheila was a good influence on Nancy. She was considerably more mature."

Carmel, as I've said, is a small town—a village, really—although it is a tourist attraction to the world. You can walk down Ocean Avenue and hear five different languages in one block. In the summer, busloads of camera-bearing tourists unload on Junipero Street near the Plaza and swarm down Ocean to spend their money and try to catch a glimpse of Clint Eastwood.

But there's a small town atmosphere here that ebbs and flows like the tide, reaching its zenith when much of the tourist traffic stops in September, and persisting through the rainy winter months when the auslanders appear only on special occasions.

A thought struck me. "Has Nancy taken up oil painting, Mrs. Blanchard?" I knew all about Nancy's principal hobby.

"Oh, no. She can't abide the smell of turpentine. Actually gives her hives, I think. No, she and Sheila met at a Bach Festival concert. They were doing BWV 243 that night, and the girls had adjoining seats. I'm afraid I had to browbeat Nancy into attending. But Sheila was a Bach enthusiast and took Nancy under her wing, so to speak."

As far as I was concerned, BWV 243 might have been a hot German automobile. (I have since learned that it refers to something called *Magnificat*.) I have eclectic musical tastes: Beethoven, Cole Porter, Stephen Sondheim, but no ear for baroque or hard rock.

The Carmel Bach Festival is a pretty important annual event, although the merchants and restaurateurs complain that the Bach fans don't spend much money and, by and large, they'd rather have more major golf tournaments and racing meets at Laguna Seca.

I told Adele that I'd snoop around and report. She agreed to leave a key to Nancy's cottage under the doormat.

Mrs. Blanchard was genuinely concerned about her daughter's situation. But, on the other hand, she had been through so many of Nancy's hide-and-seek episodes, she wasn't really what you might call distraught.

As I hung up the phone, it occurred to me that I had never even seen *Mr.* Blanchard, if he was still around. There must have *been* a Mr. Blanchard for there to be a Mrs. Blanchard and a Nancy Blanchard. Out of pure cussedness, I decided I'd check him out, too.

It wasn't the first time I'd taken on more than I could properly handle. I felt like the guy in the old vaudeville act who spins plates on long wooden rods arranged in a row. He tries to get all the plates spinning at once. But while he's approaching the last plate, the first one starts to wobble, so he has to rush back and give it another spin. The act ends either when the performer snatches all the spinning plates from the rods intact...or when they all crash to the floor in little pieces.

I wanted to keep all my plates separate and whole. So I figured I had better get face to face with Debbie Spelvin.

10

"You keep moving west till things get better or you go off the bridge."

A s I DROVE out to the Pacific Grove gate to the Seventeen Mile Drive, I thought about my earlier conversation with Armand Colbert.

I've seen Armand disturbed before. He can get pretty testy with a smartass customer or a waiter who tips a mousse on somebody. But this morning he had been more agitated than I had ever seen him. He had turned his back on me with an abrupt gesture of dismissal and shuffled unconvincingly through papers on his desk.

I had to find out more about Sheila Lord's relative on Carmel Point. I was certain that person would figure in the puzzle somewhere. But my mission now was to drive out to Pebble Beach for a chat with the Spelvins. The news that Debbie was more to Greg than a student—gossip, just gossip, maybe—and Armand's emotional display at the mention of her name were things that needed exploring.

I pulled up to the Seventeen Mile Drive gate on the Pacific Grove side. The tourist pays five bucks a car just to take the drive through some of the most beautiful private property in the world, not to mention the most challenging golf courses. But if you're visiting a resident on private business, you tell the guard to give him a call and you get in free.

After going through the formality, the guard waved me on. I had asked him to give Mr. Spelvin a ring and apparently my client responded. I headed for George's house.

The Seventeen Mile Drive is well marked for tourists. It gives them a good look at the Pebble Beach golf course, the Cypress Point golf course, the Lodge, and the Pacific Ocean. It also gives them a peek at some expensive real estate. But it makes every effort to steer them clear of a lot of the residences by encouraging them to follow the convenient yellow line.

I had visited the Spelvin place just once before, when George was sort of between wives and kept a tiny, dark-skinned lady who wore saris in the house on Santa Rita. She had George convinced she was from New Delhi, but I found out later she had grown up in Oakland and had taught in a grade school in San Leandro.

After bumbling around and taking a couple of wrong turns, I found George's place. Part Tudor and part pseudo-Spanish (to me a kind of expensive eyesore), it nestled in a grove of cypress trees, slightly uphill from the road and about thirty yards from the sixteenth tee of the Spyglass Hill golf course. It was approached by a narrow lane which led to a circular drive in front of the house.

I pressed the door bell. Waited a full minute—no response. Rang again, waited some more. Who had answered the gate-keeper's call? I was about to press the button for the third time when the door opened and Debbie Spelvin appeared.

"Hello, Riordan," she said. On her stunningly beautiful face was a brightly malicious smile. She opened the door fully and stepped back.

"You're not really surprised, are you? That I know who you are? Do you think that dumb sonofabitch George Spelvin could make any kind of a move without my knowing about it? And do you think I'm so stupid that I wouldn't find out about you the minute you started asking questions in Carmel? Come on in and have a drink."

Feeling (and probably looking) like an idiot, I stepped meekly through the door into a cool tiled hallway. Debbie led me a few feet down the hall to an archway opening into a large, sunny room furnished in early rich and hung with a couple of hundred thousand dollars' worth of art.

"Sit down, Riordan—there, on the couch. What do you drink?"

Mrs. Spelvin the sixth (or seventh?) moved to a sideboard and paused for an answer.

"No booze, please. A little Perrier, maybe? A diet Seven-Up?"

"God protect me from a reformed drunk! That's what you are, isn't it, Riordan?"

She stood there for a moment, mocking me; then turned and poured herself about an inch and a half of what looked like scotch into a tumbler and splashed in some water from a crystal pitcher. She took a thoughtful sip before opening a small refrigerator concealed behind mahogany paneling and fishing out a bottle of Perrier.

"In a glass?"

I nodded. She flipped the top off the bottle, poured its contents into another tumbler and walked across the room to me.

Debbie Spelvin was more than I had bargained for. She was tallish: five-seven, maybe, without heels. Her honey-colored hair was short but full and expensively groomed. She wore tight slacks that accented a beautiful figure and a flimsy flowered blouse that put an exclamation point to it. I could only guess about the nature of part of her lingerie but it was clear that she didn't wear any from the waist up. Not many women her age can pull that off.

What really shook me was the face: very little make-up, touch of something on the lips, natural eyebrows and lashes, a golden tan and wide green eyes.

And the poise, the control. This girl was a brand new model for George Spelvin. I had known (I think) all of the other Mrs. Spelvins over the years and they could have been stamped from the same cookie cutter. But this one did not squirm or bounce when she walked—she had the grace of a panther.

I am, I have to admit, in the neighborhood of fifty and, as private eyes go, while I'm no Buddy Ebsen, I am not Robert Wagner, either. You must understand that although I live alone and am perfectly content to do so, I have an occasional lady in for breakfast or a weekend. No saloon pick-ups. Bars don't interest me, and I only go into one in the line of duty. I have a select circle of women friends: independent ladies, professional and capable. I haven't had what you could call a love affair since I lost Helen—unless you consider my very special relationship with Reiko. But Debbie Spelvin generated in me what that old devil Henry Miller once described as "a leaping in the loins." My reverie was broken by her voice, as controlled and purposeful as her presence.

"I know that George hired you to spy on me. Well, he needn't have. We made an agreement going in: no sentiment, no strings. I give him sex—all he can handle in his usual condition—and he pays the bills. It's a kind of whorehouse relationship, Riordan. But that's all George is used to. Otherwise, he wouldn't have been screwed in so many different ways by that string of hookers he married. I hadn't counted on his bloody jealousy—he should have passed through the male menopause long before this."

She talked tough. But as I watched her face, she seemed to grow more and more vulnerable. She's role-playing, I thought, trying to project the image she thinks I expect.

She stood in the middle of that beautiful room, taking quick sips of her drink.

"Forget George." She looked hard into my eyes. "Riordan, the paper said you were there when Sheila's body was found in that crummy little cottage."

She frowned and crossed the room to the fireplace. "Sheila Lord was my friend—maybe my dearest friend. Greg Farrell...introduced us. She could have been a really good painter, but she was so mixed up, so much in pain. When I went to see her Monday afternoon, I thought she might be about to snap out of it. She seemed reasonably cheerful. She was looking forward to the Bach Festival concert that night."

It seemed only natural that the circle completed itself. That day's quota of surprises had been used up when Armand told me about Debbie and Greg. But all I could do at this point was sit and stare at this beautiful woman and try to remember the morning a couple of days earlier when I had been roused from my innocent sleep to go look at a pale bloody corpse.

When I left the Spelvin place an hour or so later, I was completely turned around about Debbie. Even the name was wrong. It was a cheerleader name, a Valley Girl name. And this was a strong, intelligent woman who had been knocked around a lot since leaving her unpleasant home in Chicago. She was beautiful, so she could always find work—of a sort. She had no office skills and modeling was chancy. So she went to work as a hostess for a private club. The job paid pretty well and got her into a spread in a girly magazine (which we all bought, you understand, because it contained stories by Nabokov and articles on Henry Kissinger). But because she wouldn't take her pants off, she was just one of six girls on a page.

"Why do men go for those gynecology shots, Riordan?" She shot me an angry glance. Then, more quietly: "Why do some women just love to pose for 'em?"

Debbie told me all, quite freely. Her initial hostility seemed to wear off shortly after she began talking about Sheila Lord. I was sitting on a couch that was altogether too soft and expensive. She moved about the room with that animal grace, and I had to fight to focus my attention on what she was saying as my eyes followed that wonderful body.

"There are some things that happened in Chicago, Riordan, that I won't tell you about. They're none of your business, anyhow. But I got sick of the place and headed out for California. Isn't that what everybody does? You keep moving west until things get better or you go off the bridge. I tried modeling agencies. Never saw so many gorgeous girls in my life, most of them years younger than I was. Finally I got a job as a restaurant hostess in Marin. George came in one night with a cute little red-headed ingenue wearing lavender eye shadow. Boobs out to here. I guess he'd had her around a shade too long because he managed to get my phone number and . . . ."

She perched on the arm of a chair opposite me. It was as close as she came to sitting down.

"Please believe me, Riordan. George is not a bad guy. He's a little rich kid who never grew up. But he's over sixty and drinks too much and he's running out of gas. And I am not a quick easy lay for any barroom punk!"

I could fall in love with this woman, I thought. Maybe I already had. Don't just stare at her shirt, dummy! It was time to leave and I didn't want to go. There's an inevitable conclusion here somewhere.

This is not a biography of the current Mrs. Spelvin. Aside from her friendship with the murdered Miss Lord, Debbie had another revelation for me: the identity of Sheila's relative at the Point. I asked her. It was the only question I had left.

I think I held her warm soft hand a bit too long as I said goodbye, and her perfume lingered with me all the way into Monterey.

11

"...we're a pretty tight crowd at Pebble."

I DROVE BACK to the office. Reiko wasn't there. I sat back in my newly acquired foam-padded swivel chair and planned the cruel, cutting remarks I would make when she showed up.

"Where've you been?"

Reiko breezed into the office with a lined yellow legal pad under her arm. It was four o'clock and I had been waiting for her more than an hour. I had thought of a number of nasty things to say, but I'm afraid I must have dozed off.

"The library."

"Reading books?"

"Reading newspapers."

"Reiko, I know I owe you money but I do expect you to hang around the office in case some business walks in or the telephone rings."

"Nobody's going to walk in 'cause they don't know you're here. And you're not in the yellow pages yet, so nobody's going to call. And if somebody *does* call, we've got that answering gadget on the phone. So stuff it."

As usual, she had me stopped.

I became my usual humble self. "Why have you been reading newspapers, Reiko-san?"

"I do your filing, right? So I know all about Nancy Blanchard and her problems. And that old dragon of a mother tried to bull-doze me this morning, right?"

"Right. So. . .?"

"Something clicked after she called. Something about Harding Blanchard, the old broad's husband, Nancy's father. I remembered that there was a big story seven or eight years ago about him. I looked it up. He disappeared, Pat. One day he's a respected member of the community, a Pebble Beach yachtsman. Next day, he's gone without a trace."

As Reiko related the details, I learned that Harding Blanchard had disappeared about a month before George Spelvin had called me on Adele Blanchard's behalf, about sixteen-year-old Nancy's first runaway. Why hadn't George told me about the missing Mr. Blanchard?

I confronted him with the question at the Lodge an hour later. He was not really sober but still fairly lucid.

"Look, Riordan, we're a pretty tight crowd at Pebble."

I was amused at his adjective. It described George a lot of the time.

"We look after our own—like the Mormons or the Chinese. When Hardy Blanchard took off, nobody was that surprised. You know Adele. It's all her money, you know, her family's money. Hardy had a good name but no bucks, understand. But he was a nice guy. I'm glad he got away."

"Didn't anybody have an idea about where he went? Or what finally made him take off?"

"Nobody around here asked, Pat. Hardy had been playing around a little. God knows Adele is hard to take. I've often wondered how she got pregnant with Nancy. Osmosis, maybe. I don't think I ever heard anybody say so, but most of us figured he just ran away with some girl he met in a Carmel bar. We *hoped* he ran away. And we hope he's living in Hawaii under another name."

He paused. "Funny thing, though. Adele never wanted to find him. The word that he was gone leaked out through the household staff. When the police got hold of it, they did everything they could. After a couple of months, they just gave up. And Adele didn't push 'em. She hadn't paid that much attention to Hardy, so she just carried on as if nothing had happened. Like he'd been invisible to her for years, so he might as well stay invisible."

I drove back to Monterey and caught Reiko just as she was locking up. I felt a little sheepish, so I offered to take her to dinner. This presents a problem.

There is a throw-away gazette aimed at tourists and circulated weekly around the Monterey Peninsula that purports to be a restaurant guide, among other things. It lists alphabetically all the eating places in the area, classifies them according to cuisine and provides a brief description, including price range. I used to know the guy who published the thing, as well as the other little local weekly, known for generations as the *Carmel Pine Cone*.

"Al, how do you keep up with all the restaurants?" I once asked him. "Some of 'em don't last three months. Some of 'em keep the same name but change hands and maybe chefs every six months. They switch their hours, their prices and their menus. I recommend a place to somebody, he goes and it's out of business. Or, in the popular fiction of the area, they're 'closed for remodeling,' or 'on vacation, back in January.'"

"We can't keep track if they don't tell us. If *somebody* doesn't tell us. That's usually what happens. Somebody calls up and chews my ass, and I know another restaurant has gone belly-up."

I wanted to take Reiko out for a nice, gourmet-type dinner to show her my gratitude for coming down here in the first place and my appreciation for digging up the dirt on Harding Blanchard in the second place. But what I was facing was a kind of alimentary Russian roulette.

We could wander around Carmel looking at menus posted outside for the tourists' inspection. One can see these visitors everywhere: men and women in their plaid shorts and pale, knobby knees above red sox and blue Nikes, shivering bravely in the fog, having arrived in this tourist mecca with the myth of sunny California in their hearts.

"This used to be a good one, honey."

I dragged Reiko up a flight of stairs to a restaurant I had known for years in a couple of different locations. It had a Swiss ambience and served Swiss-German food, tasty and well-presented but not heavy with dumplings and noodles. I was pleased and relieved to find Inge still in the dining room, receiving, seating, and serving, while Heinz did his one-man balancing act in the kitchen.

"Have the veal piccata. Nobody fixes it like Heinz."

The piccata at this place is composed of slices of real veal—the white stuff—and zucchini, dipped in a light egg batter and sauteed in a lemony sauce. It's served with nice fresh green vegetables *al dente*.

Reiko had her nose in the menu.

"No fish. Too bad."

"Honey, they've got chicken, they've got a veggie plate, whatever."

"I saw a place across the street. They've got fish."

I made my apologies to Inge, grasped Reiko firmly by the elbow, and maneuvered her briskly out the door and down the stairs.

Shortly thereafter I was able to watch my beloved, but exasperating, secretary-assistant-keeper wolf down a huge slab of poached Monterey Bay salmon, half a pound of hand-cut french fries, and an intimidating portion of cherry cheesecake. I had a little calamari, sautéed in garlic butter. Calamari, my friends, is a code word universally used on the west coast to keep people from realizing that they're eating squid. Cooked a certain way it tastes almost like abalone, an overrated univalue whose price per ounce now rivals the Krugerrand.

While Reiko focused her attention on the cheesecake, I looked around the restaurant. In a shadowy corner sat a dark-skinned man dressed all in black, with glistening silver hair. Without doubt he was watching us.

I leaned across the table to Reiko.

"See that white-haired man in the corner? He's keeping an eye on us."

Reiko glanced over casually.

"Oh, him. Don't worry, Riordan, he works for Sheila Lord's aunt."

12

"Pardon me, I am looking for employment."

I DROVE REIKO to her apartment in Pacific Grove in silence. I hadn't yet had the nerve to ask her how she knew about Sheila Lord's Carmel Point relative. She seemed disinclined to explain herself, so I walked her to her door, pecked her on the cheek, and went home.

Next morning, I showered and shaved and arrived at the office early. Reiko was there, doing whatever she did with her personal computer.

I took a position squarely in front of her desk.

"How did you know about Sheila Lord's aunt and that shifty little guy with the white hair who, you insist, works for her?"

She allowed herself a sigh of pity and resignation. "My Uncle Shiro—you know, our landlord, the guy who owns this building—has, among other enterprises, the largest residential gardening service on the Peninsula. Thirty trucks he has, and does he ever make money. Anyway, I called him to see if he had any information we could use about the Lord case. He put out the word to his drivers, and one guy who works the Carmel Point area reported that he knew Sheila Lord, sort of casually, through mutual friends, and that he looked after her aunt's shrubbery. Presto, the aunt; double-presto, the aunt's only live-in employee, the white-haired guy we saw last night. Uncle Shiro's boy described him to a T. He's not big, but he's pretty scary."

That's Reiko. She's pretty scary herself, sometimes.

*   *   *

About a year after Helen was killed, Reiko came into my life.

I was sitting in what passed for my San Francisco office, in one of the oldest buildings on Market Street. It had survived the '06 Quake, but later succumbed to the madness that has replaced all those fine old buildings with high rises, in pure defiance of the San Andreas Fault. I was badly hung over, trying to decide whether to slash my wrists or pay the rent. My wife's insurance money (a considerable amount) had been pissed away almost literally, considering the effect of booze on my kidneys.

The door was ajar, as it almost always was. My morning headaches made even the clicking of the latch painful, and in my customary evening stupor, I would simply forget to close the door behind me as I left.

"Pardon me, I am looking for employment. Is your secretary ill or does your office always look this way?"

I had been staring out the window at the tip of the Ferry Building that stood bravely about the Embarcadero Freeway. When I swung my squeaky swivel chair around and allowed my eyes to focus on the doorway, I saw her.

About five-foot-nothing, petite but compact, glistening black hair parted on a sort of diagonal and pulled tightly back into a ponytail, a faint, quizzical smile on her face: this was Reiko.

"Maybe you didn't hear me. I am looking for employment. I got sick of answering classified ads which took me halfway around the Bay. So I decided to be systematic. I am working your building from top to bottom. It saves energy. I take the elevator all the way up and work my way down the stairs. Doesn't that suggest efficiency?"

I nodded stupidly. She stood in the doorway, surveying every corner of my grubby room. She was a cool little woman with a face like a doll in a Chinatown shop window. To my bloodshot eyes, she appeared to be somewhere between fifteen and forty, and she had a low, throaty voice that was smooth as gelato.

"I am a graduate of San Jose State, with a major in English and a minor in sociology. My mother insisted that any job I could get with an English major would either be immoral or underpaid or both. So she sent me to business school after college."

She sniffed a superior sniff. "I see you have no computer. Do you keep books? Do you have correspondence? Do you make any money? What the hell do you do, anyhow?"

I was bedazzled. My headache disappeared. I wished I had taken time to shave. I fumbled in my top drawer for the tiny bottle of breath-freshener.

"I—I'm, ah, a private investigator. You know, like Sam Spade or Philip Marlowe or . . . ."

"What does a private investigator investigate? And who are Mr. Spade and Mr. Marlowe?"

I'm sure now that she was kidding me. But that morning I was pretty foggy.

"Uh, ah . . . a private investigator investigates anything anybody hires him to investigate. The, ah, operative word is *private*. My name is Riordan. For now, you can forget about the other guys."

I was beginning to come to life. All of a sudden. This small woman with the positive attitude was striking a new chord inside me. Since Helen's death, my life had taken on the mahogany shade of the barrooms I had been living in.

"You need somebody pretty badly, don't you, Mr. Riordan?"

Her eyes narrowed and she frowned. "You've been suffering, haven't you? You've got great bags under your eyes, and I think you feel sorry for yourself. There's a stale smell of whiskey here and you're wearing a dirty shirt. That's an expensive suit, but it looks awful. Can you afford to hire me?"

In years to follow, I got used to the way words came tumbling out of Reiko's mouth. I came to appreciate the wonderful clarity of her thoughts as they cascaded forth. I have never ceased to be amazed at her intuition. But at this remembered moment, I was confused.

"How much money do you need?" I asked, confusedly.

Her head made a quarter turn to the right, and she peeked at me from the corners of her eyes. She clasped her hands demurely at her waist.

"My God, I don't know," I said out loud.

I think I sounded a little hysterical. But I was telling the truth. I'd had a couple of girls in the office over the years. One was a huge redhead with an unbelievable bosom who smoked long cigarettes and chewed Juicy Fruit gum at the same time. The other was an elderly lady—friend of a friend of Helen's—who was more than slightly deaf, and sometimes did not hear the phone. I couldn't remember what I paid them. So how was I supposed to know what to offer this feisty little college graduate whose mother had no respect for English majors?

She stood silent, looking at me obliquely. After a long moment, she spoke: "My name is Reiko Masuda. My mother named me Denise. She also named my brothers Derek and Kevin. We all have Japanese middle names. I use mine. I am twenty-five years old and I don't fool around."

There was a brief flash in those penetrating black eyes that I was to become very familiar with in later times, a sort of controlled defiance that I learned to admire.

"I think you need me, Mr. Riordan. More than I need you. That is why I will work for you."

"Eight-fifty a month?"

"Nine hundred."

"Done. When?"

She hesitated. "Today is Thursday. I have a studio apartment in the Richmond district in a building my aunt owns. But I must spend this weekend with Mama in San Jose. Monday OK?"

"Fine, fine, Reiko. I'll try to get things a little tidied up for you. And if you do the kind of job I think you can do, I'll see about more money in a month or so."

She smiled broadly for the first time. "Don't worry about it Riordan-san. My grandpa farmed strawberries for twenty years in what is now most of Silicon Valley. We're loaded. See you Monday."

And she glided sideways out the door.

13

"Get in my way and I'll run your ass back to San Francisco."

I T WAS TIME to find out more about Sheila Lord's aunt.

In a small community where a sixty-year-old, termite-infested lean-to can cost $200,000, money becomes unreal. As a kid, I used to get a three-dip ice cream cone for a nickel. The ice cream place on Ocean Avenue gets three bucks for a pint, and it's going out of business. And cones are about to become illegal in Carmel.

Carmel Point contains some of the most discouragingly expensive property on the Monterey Peninsula. It's a small corner of land on the southwest edge of Carmel. It lies between the great white Carmel beach that the tourists know and the quieter beach on a small bay that is bounded on the south by Point Lobos and diluted by fresh water from the Santa Lucia Mountains via the Carmel River. Most of the Point is unincorporated territory, a condition that does not provide a tax advantage but does make the residents eligible for mail delivery. The Old Ranch is in the county, too, which accounts for the fact that the Monterey County sheriff's office was handling the investigation of Sheila Lord's murder.

Debbie Spelvin had told me that Lord's aunt, Felicia Montalvo, had bought the house on the Point several years before Sheila moved down from San Jose. It was at a time when property was not nearly so expensive as it is now, but even then it must have cost her a bundle. The rumor was thatMontalvo had laid it all down on the

71

realtor's desk in thousand dollar bills. But you know how these real estate people are—inclined to dramatize a bit.

I approached the house on foot. On the short, curving streets of the Point, I am never quite sure where I am. The tourist takes Scenic Road from the foot of Ocean all the way around the Point and is unaware of these quiet, wealthy streets, a block or two from the Pacific. General "Vinegar Joe" Stilwell lived here. Robinson Jeffers, who spent his poetic life writing about the central California coast country from here to Big Sur, was one of the first to build here, a house made of stone from the ocean shore. There was nothing here then but scrub and sand. Jeffers planted trees and built with his own hands a brooding stone tower. It's still here.

Debbie had described Aunt Felicia's house to me and had given me instructions for finding it. I had parked by a grove of tall trees that I thought I could find again and started to walk. After a couple of embarrassing wrong doors, I finally located the place at the junction of two unmarked streets. Its two stories loomed over its rambling ranch-style neighbors and the side facing the ocean was mostly glass on the upper level, including what appeared to be an enormous skylight.

As I lifted my hand to knock on the door, I reflected again that I was not getting paid for this. George Spelvin was paying me—and he could well afford it—to find out if his wife was playing around. It occurred to me that I could get in big trouble with the sheriff if I didn't pass along to him all the information I had picked up about Sheila Lord. Before I could touch the door, however, it opened and Detective Sergeant Balestreri walked into me.

"I'm sorry!" he said, before he recognized me. When he got a good look, though, he grasped me firmly by the shirt front and led me ten paces down the stone walkway from the house.

"Riordan, I strongly suspect that you are going to get in my way. Aside from being a witness after the fact, you have no interest in this case. Unless...."

He stepped back and let go of my shirt. "Unless you have something to tell me that'll help, I'll ask you—no, *order* you to back off right now."

Quickly, I blurted out all of the pertinent information—which was just about everything I had learned since the day before. Balestreri nodded occasionally, staring past my left ear. At one point, he flipped a small notebook out of his shirt pocket and made a few notes with a chewed pencil stub.

When I finished, he looked at me with a trace of a smile and said: "Guess it's impossible to keep you clear of this case, Riordan. Too many of your friends might be involved. And you don't get much excitement in the kind of work you usually do. You won't get anything out of the old lady in there, though. She's a cold customer. Hard to get her to admit she ever had a niece."

His eyes became menacing again. "Have your fun, Riordan. But make sure you keep me posted on anything you find out. Get in my way and I'll run your ass back to San Francisco."

He pronounced the name with long, flat vowels: "Sa-an Fra-an-cisco." People from the City normally say something like "Saffer-cisco." John O'Hara spelled it that way in a short story long ago. He was trying to suggest a drunk saying it. Maybe he was telling us something.

Balestreri walked down the curving stone strip and crossed the street to his car. I must have been preoccupied not to have noticed it as I approached the house. Maybe I was thinking of the enchanting Mrs. Spelvin.

I turned back to the house. What the hell. . . I've got this far. I took a deep breath and knocked.

Almost immediately the door opened, and a mild-looking man in a black turtleneck gazed inquiringly at me. He had very dark skin despite classic Anglo-Saxon features, light eyes, and carefully combed and sprayed white hair. There was a flicker of recognition in his eyes, and I'm sure I must have returned the signal.

"Yes?" he said or asked, as the case may be.

"I would like to speak to Mrs. Montalvo, if it's possible." I tried to be charming.

"It is *Miss* Montalvo, sir, and I will see if she will receive you. Your name and business?" This was routine. He knew who I was.

"My name is Riordan and I'm investigating the death of her niece." That just might have been a pretty dumb thing to say.

"Are you with that policeman?"

He pointed across the street at Balestreri's car, just pulling away. "No. Well, yes, in a way. We...we're working together."

A high-pitched, reedy, commanding voice came from somewhere above us.

"Let him come up. That sergeant broke my concentration. This person can't do any more harm."

14

"I need no one, sir, you see."

THE WHITE-HAIRED man led me to a narrow, carpeted stairway and backed away. Before starting up, I took a deliberate look around. In the hall and the two rooms I could see, the walls were covered with oil paintings of all sizes and shapes, from about waist-high to the ceiling. They all looked very good to me, very expensive. But the effect was overpowering. Too much.

I climbed the stairs and found myself in a huge studio whose walls on three sides were also thickly hung with paintings. The wall towards the ocean side of the house was glass, and at least twelve feet high. Heavy drapes were gathered at either side of the glass wall to draw against the late afternoon sun. Canvases were stacked everywhere, and the smell of artist's oils was heavy.

There were racks of completed paintings; empty frames were piled on furniture. These were fancy frames, too, unlike those used by most of my hungry artist friends, who choose the simple box type gallery frame consisting of four strips of painted wood tacked around the canvas.

In the center of the room stood a large, sturdy, professional easel holding a canvas that must have measured at least a yard each way. Before the canvas on a high stool sat Felicia Montalvo.

The first thing that impressed me about her was her long, curved, aristocratic nose. It was a masterpiece. Somewhere in her lineage must have been a Spanish grandee. The nose could have been more impressive, though, had it not been for her small black, glittering eyes. The mouth was firm and full, the chin and jaw line perhaps too strong. It was a face that needed a little relief, some softening. But it didn't get it from the hair which was iron gray and pulled straight back, tightly and severely. So much tension was exerted on the skin of the face that the eyes looked Oriental and the forehead incredibly smooth for a lady of her years. Maybe that was the idea.

Miss Montalvo sat easily on the stool, one foot on the floor, the heel of the other hooked behind a cross-piece. Her back was straight and she radiated an aristocratic air, palette in left hand, brush in right, poised before the canvas. She had to be at least seventy, but you weren't going to get her to admit it.

"I have been asked by some of Sheila's friends to do as much as I can to find out who killed her and why, Miss Montalvo. I am a—uh—private investigator."

I lied a little there. I was into this thing mainly because of my own reckless curiosity. It felt a little funny to add that last line, but the formidable Aunt Felicia had been looking at me as though I should be skewered with a pin in a specimen case.

She dabbed some paint onto the canvas with deliberation.

"Sir, the policeman who was here before asked a lot of questions I did not choose to answer. I do not choose to answer yours. I will say only this: for the past three years I have supported my niece, not because I liked her particularly, but because—despite her weakness of character—she showed promise of becoming a real artist. The fact that she was my sister's only child meant nothing. I couldn't stand my sister, either."

She had stared at her painting during this speech. Then she applied just a touch of the same color to another part of the surface and stood up to look at her work.

"Are you a...professional artist, Miss Montalvo? Are all of the things downstairs and here...yours?" I was having trouble making conversation.

"Do I make money from my painting, sir? No, I do not. I am perhaps the best technician in this dreadfully arty little town. But I am a copyist, sir, a copyist! I paint other paintings, and many of mine are superior to the originals."

She turned the easel towards me, and I saw what she had been painting: a beautiful, brightly colored, rainy cityscape—a real grabber I would love to own. Clipped to the top of the easel was the identical painting in miniature from the brochure of a French artist whose works hung in a rather pretentious gallery on Sixth.

She turned those piercing eyes on me again. "I get pleasure in two ways, sir. I can surround myself with the very best art at the cost of only the raw materials. And I have the satisfaction of having improved on some expensive pieces. This one, for example. I have studied this painting in the gallery. I need only the reproduction to remind me of what I must paint."

I was impressed. Probably only the original artist could tell his own work from this copy. It was shade for shade, stroke for stroke. But the way Felicia said "sir" gave me chills.

"I don't need the money, sir, or I could undoubtedly make a good living at counterfeiting. Then, however, I should have to turn my efforts to artists of great name and repute, and go to all the trouble of aging them falsely. Fortunately, I am in semi-retirement from several very lucrative businesses, and I am able to indulge my dishonest little hobby while living in the comfort I deserve."

She leaned towards me with a tight-lipped smile.

"I need no one, sir, you see. I have beauty all around me. I have the best to eat and drink. And I haven't had an orgasm for thirty years."

15

"I think I might have killed Sheila Lord."

THE KEY was under the doormat, but nothing in Nancy Blanchard's cottage suggested a struggle—or anything else, for that matter. The furniture was all in place, the bed neatly made.

Adele had had the place professionally decorated, and it was charming in its way, but too chi-chi for me: all mauves and grays and muted pinks. The stuff was expensive; that was to be expected. Nothing but the best for Adele Blanchard's daughter. But an antique wood-burning range in the living room, supporting the TV?

I poked around aimlessly, looking in drawers, opening closets, trying to find something—anything—that would tell me what happened to Nancy.

I had just opened a bottle of diet soda when I heard a key in the front door. I came out of the kitchen to find Nancy Blanchard looking puzzled and not a little angry.

When she saw me, her face relaxed. "Pat Riordan, you old sonofabitch. I might have known. I saw the car outside, but *everybody* in Carmel drives a Mercedes these days."

Nancy is a small girl, not as short as Reiko, but not much taller and not nearly as sturdy. She has a pinched, bird-like look with pointed little features, small bones and breasts. Although she looks frail and vulnerable, she is a veritable tigress in the sack, according to more than one of her numerous lovers. I swear I don't know first-hand, although Nancy has never been shy about inviting me into her bed. I declined, of course, for professional reasons.

"OK, let's see, Nancy. You went to San Francisco to shop. You saw some old friends and decided to stay a few days. And you didn't tell Mama."

Nancy's face clouded. I had never seen that expression before.

"I went to San Francisco...not to shop. And not with some guy."

She sat wearily on her couch and clutched a throw pillow to her chest. "I've been going to a doctor, Pat. A shrink. For a long time. You know I've done a lot of crazy things in the past. I've always had this gnawing feeling that there's something wrong in my head. Then when I heard about Sheila Lord...."

Nancy looked very small and helpless, and tears glistened in her eyes. "It was an awful shock, Pat. Sheila was everything I'm not. She was talented, she was kind and gentle and loving. And I've never been worth a diddley-shit."

I moved to the couch and put an arm around her. Nancy curled up in the fetal position and covered her face with a hand.

"Mother could never see me as anything but a bad little kid. Even after I grew up and she hired you to chase after me and bring me back here. My life has had nightmares in it, Pat. Times when I seemed to black out, lose all sense of reality.

"Now I think I might have killed Sheila Lord."

She burst into convulsive sobs, and tears streamed down her face. She was a scared little girl, and now I knew why.

When the sobbing began to subside, I asked her the obvious question: "Why would you kill Sheila? And how? When did you see her last? She's been out of circulation for months."

"I don't know, I don't know. We had kept in touch. We were supposed to meet that Monday night for a Bach Festival concert. I remember leaving here to pick her up. Then nothing—until I woke up in my bed around noon on Tuesday. I had a terrible nightmare that night. I saw Sheila dead in her casket. But the undertakers had left this big kitchen knife buried in her chest...and when they tried to close the casket, the lid wouldn't go down."

She shuddered. "I took a couple of tranquilizers to steady me, but they didn't seem to do much good. I had a cup of coffee and walked down to Ocean Avenue. When I saw the headline in the *Herald* about Sheila, I screamed right in front of the drugstore! People pretended not to notice."

Nancy seemed to be gaining control. She giggled. "I remember this old shaggy dog, tethered outside the store, looked up at me with his big dark eyes and whimpered. I knelt down and petted him, and he licked my hand. Just then everything seemed normal again, and I was just little Nancy Blanchard walking in the rare July sunshine on the streets of Carmel."

She fell silent. I sat with her for a while until she seemed to relax. Then I phoned Adele and told her that her only child was back... and needed help.

16

It was just at that point that somebody slugged me from behind.

ADELE ARRIVED from her condo on the hill, and I took off.

It seemed unlikely to me that Nancy Blanchard killed Sheila, no matter what sort of mental problems Nancy was having. Nancy might be neurotic, but I've never known her to be violent. And I couldn't be sure she wasn't taking some sort of medication, legally prescribed by the shrink in San Francisco, which would account for her blackout. Nancy is compulsive. She is the kind of person who thinks that if one pill is good, five are a hell of a lot better.

What, then? Or who? The dope in Sheila didn't indicate a habit. Aunt Felicia seemed to have coldly disengaged herself from the whole affair. The white-haired man made me nervous. Debbie Spelvin had cast a spell on me. And George was probably drunk at the Lodge.

A shaft of sunlight penetrated the fog as I drove down from the Woods. I pulled up at my cottage and got on the phone to Balestreri.

"Sergeant, I'm sure you went over the scene of the crime after I left, didn't you?"

"Sure. Why?"

"The painting. You saw the painting on the floor?"

"I am neither stupid nor blind, Riordan. I saw the painting. I noted that it probably came close to duplicating what you saw when you opened the door. It was photographed by our boy and will be used in evidence when we find somebody to prosecute."

"Where is it now?"

"Where? Right where it was originally. On the easel. In the corner. In the cottage."

"And the cottage is locked?"

"Tight as we could lock it. Sheriff's seal on every opening. Yellow tape around the building."

I thanked him and was about to hang up, when he yelled at me: "Hey, what's this all about?"

"Just interested, Sergeant. Did you notice anything unusual about the painting?"

"Hell, no. A painting. I'm no judge of its quality. No signature on it."

"Well, thanks again. You know where I am if you need me."

For a few minutes after I hung up the phone, I just stared out the window. An Irish setter was lying in the middle of Santa Rita Street outside my cottage. I think he was staring back at me.

That painting bothered me. I hadn't really taken a good look at it, and could barely remember it now. But one thing came back with a rush. That morning—which now seemed so long ago—the painting was wet with paint the color of blood. I had to see it again as soon as possible.

The fog was coming in swiftly and it was going to be heavy. That was good. I had made up my mind that I was going to take a close look at the painting. I would have to go out to the Old Ranch late at night, under cover of the blessed fog, and somehow get into Sheila Lord's cottage. If I found anything I could tell Balestreri later. If I didn't, there was no need for him to know I had returned to the scene of the crime.

As I have said before, all the buildings at the Ranch are pretty old, and although they have been slicked up and painted in recent years, a competent professional burglar would regard any of them as a piece of cake. But the grounds are always well-lighted, and there's generally somebody prowling around. The restaurant does very good business and the bar keeps legal hours.

Just before two in the morning, I drove over, parked behind the

Mission, and walked up to the wide curve where Dolores Street turns into something else. Clutching a small plastic flashlight and a Polaroid camera, I turned onto the tennis court road and waited on a wooden bench for the last of the bar crowd to leave. The cars filed out of the Ranch gate, a group of five or six, followed by two and three and one. The night grew quiet.

I walked up the hill and looked over towards the restaurant. A light or two. Somebody left behind for clean-up. I had to do it now. As I moved down the hill to the cottage, the fog was thickening and the only light came from a single yellow bulb above the door of each building. The silence was unbroken, except for the twigs and eucalyptus pods that crunched under my feet.

It was plain when I reached Sheila's cottage that getting in without leaving the mark of a break-in was not going to be easy. The yellow tape was there, glowing in the dark, all around the small house. The front door was sealed in several places with heavy adhesive plastic seals. I don't know quite what I had expected, but I very nearly gave up the whole operation right then. The place was unguarded, however. (After all, what was the use of squandering manpower? Who really cared about Sheila Lord's murder?) I crept around the cottage in a kind of Groucho stoop, examining the windows, all of which were locked, some sealed with twenty years of paint as well. I reached the kitchen door. Either the sheriff's men had forgotten about it or they just didn't consider it important. There were no seals here.

Maybe I could open it with a credit card. I've seen people on TV doing that. No, these were very old locks: the key moved a deadbolt into a hole, simple and effective. I pulled out my keys and felt them in the dark. Nothing here that could possibly work. In desperation, I leaned over the yellow tape and grasped the door-knob. As I touched it, the door swung quietly inward, and in a second I was inside.

I will never mention this to Balestreri, I thought. No reason for him to know that one of his boys blew it. But I smiled in the blackness and felt a little smug.

No point in wasting time. I went immediately to the living room, barking my shins on several unremembered pieces of furniture. I cannot explain why I did not use the flashlight clutched in my right hand to avoid the furniture. I did use it to find the painting. It was on the easel in the corner, where it had been when I walked in the door the first morning.

I directed the light beam onto the picture. It had changed, I thought, although I could not tell how. I reached out and touched it with the tip of my right index finger. Dry.

I swung up the Polaroid which had been dangling from my neck, thumping me on the chest. Aiming with the aid of the flashlight, I took a shot of the painting. Shoving the developing picture in my pocket, I leaned closer to the painting. I ran a fingernail across the surface and was not too surprised when some of the paint flaked off.

It was just at that point that somebody slugged me from behind. I have a faint impression that I heard something and was about to turn my head when the blow was struck. Or maybe I got far enough around to see something, because later I got these little flashes of a face I ought to know.

I was out about fifteen minutes, no more. When I came round, I knew right away where I was and that I was in trouble. I groped for the flashlight and confirmed what I suspected even before my eyes opened. The painting was gone. So was the Polaroid print which had been in my pocket.

I pulled myself up and sat carefully in one of the two lumpy living room chairs. My head hurt like hell with each slight movement, so I tried to remain very still. My mind was functioning in tiny flashes. All sorts of impressions, out of sequence, flew through my head. The murder of Sheila Lord didn't make sense at all. Naked but not raped. Full of heroin but not an addict, not an OD. The picture? Was it Sheila? Could have been; coloring was right. Damn? Why hadn't I looked more closely? Whoever slugged me had my Polaroid print.

It was quiet as death. Sitting in that cottage, aching and addled, I felt suspended in space. A little buzz of fear began at the back of my neck and sharpened my headache. I managed to stand up with great pain and, forgetting caution, flashlighted my way out of the little house.

Very slowly, I walked back to my car and eased myself behind the wheel. I sat still for another quarter of an hour, my mind galloping off in all directions. It was like getting a slug of Demerol, that made you goofy but didn't kill the pain. The next ten minutes are lost forever in the computer I carry between my ears. I was somehow back in my house. I managed to crawl up the stairs and onto the bed. I closed my eyes and, just as I was drifting off, remembered something about not falling asleep immediately after a blow on the head, because of concussion. But it was too late, and I was tired, and at that precise moment, I really didn't give a damn.

17

"There's got to be something about that picture that answers an important question."

WHEN I OPENED my eyes, it was mid-morning. Reiko was sitting on my bed, holding my hand. On her face was an unaccustomed expression of worry. She leaned down and kissed me gently on the cheek.

"How'd you get in here?"

"Picked the lock, dummy," she said. "Now tell me how you got into this condition. There's blood on the back of your head and you're sticking to the pillow."

The greater likelihood was that I had just left the door open in my semi-conscious state, but I let it go.

"Why did you come here, anyhow?"

"Balestreri has been trying to reach you all morning. He called the office first. Then here. Then he called me back and said you didn't answer. Then I called here and you didn't answer. So I figured you were either hurt or drunk. Either way you needed help. So I came."

I sat up slowly and swung my legs over the side of the bed. The pillow came up with my head, and Reiko peeled it away. It was like stripping off a large piece of adhesive tape, only more painful.

"Run on over to the office, honey. Mind the store. We need all the work we can get. I'll tell you later about last night. When I can remember more."

After Reiko left, I took a quick, hot shower to get the dried blood out of my hair. My finger tips told me that the cut in my scalp was of little consequence. A cup of instant coffee tasted awful, but made me feel just a shade better. I called Balestreri.

"Where the hell have you been? Sheila Lord's cottage was broken into last night. Do you know anything about that, Riordan?"

He was angry. It must have been intuitive. He had no way of knowing I was in the cottage. But he had great instincts.

I replied in an injured tone: "Christ, Sergeant! Just why are you so hot at me? I'm a poor city boy, mixed up in a mess that's not going to make me a dime. . . ."

"Do you know what they took, Riordan? The painting. That's all. They came there for the painting, entered and left by the back door."

"I am not responsible for the failure of your staff people to lock doors. . . ."

"It was locked! We didn't think it was necessary to nail the place shut or padlock it. But we locked it with the regular keys. Dammit, Riordan, there's got to be something about that picture that answers an important question. Good thing we photographed it."

Eureka! I had forgotten that the law had taken pictures.

"Balestreri, can you get a blow-up of that picture—the photo of the painting?"

"I could."

"Have it enlarged as close to the original size as you can. How long will it take?"

"Why the hell should I do this for you, Riordan? I am not going to play second banana to you in this investigation."

I could see those unblinking eyes getting hard and the mouth drawing into a firm, straight line. He had his back up.

I softened up a little. "I'm sorry. Got carried away for a minute. Honest to God, I have a really good reason. It's hard to explain over the phone. But, please, Sergeant, get the blow-up. If I can't justify it, you can kick my ass out of Monterey County."

"You just wrote it, Riordan. It'll maybe take a couple of days to get the job done."

"Call me, Sergeant, as soon as the blow-up is in your hands."

18

"Throw away the stick and give him your wallet."

IT WAS TIME to do some prowling. Felicia Montalvo's white-haired lad had been checking me out. I had caught glimpses of him twice since he followed Reiko and me into the fish restaurant. It was time for me to check on him. Reiko's uncle's boy had told her that there were some pretty interesting rumors floating around about him.

I never carry a gun. I don't like guns. They're necessary, I will allow, for police officers who have to use them in self-defense. God knows, plenty of bad guys and crazies can get them and use them.

But a handgun is meant for only one thing: to put a hole in somebody. I had enough of putting holes in people in Korea.

Helen used to urge me to get some sort of little concealable firearm in case somebody I was watching got nasty. Reiko would probably have me carry a submachine gun. But I always stand fast.

I make one concession about weapons. Years ago, Helen bought me a blackthorn stick in a little Irish shop in Los Gatos. She said it was the nearest thing to a shillelagh she could find. It's a hard, knobby, ugly thing, and I carry it when I feel that some trouble might develop. With a walking stick I can either look like a cripple and avoid a confrontation, or swing it on somebody if I'm trapped.

I asked an old friend of mine, a retired Army colonel, what he thought about the blackthorn stick as a weapon.

"Well, if a guy comes at you with a knife, aim it for his throat. That can kill 'im. If somebody comes at you with a brick, get him in the balls. That'll sure stop 'im. Then, if somebody pulls a gun on you...."

He paused with eyebrows lifted.

"Yeah?"

"Throw away the stick and give him your wallet."

So it was with some trepidation that I determined to follow Felicia's wiry little henchman to see what he did when he was not answering the doorbell for the old lady.

I parked by what was left of Robinson Jeffers's original grove of trees and observed the Montalvo house about a block away.

At length the white-haired man came out and got into a faded blue Camaro parked discreetly against a high hedge that fronted Felicia's property. Carmel, surprisingly, is full of old automobiles, most of which have ruined finishes from the salt air, and permanent dents from running through blind, unmarked intersections. When you eliminate the tourist cars, you're down to two kinds: hopeless junkers on the one hand and the Rolls-Mercedes-Ferrari group on the other. Natives hereabouts call the Mercedes the "Carmel Volkswagen."

White-hair pulled out slowly and turned right, heading for town. At Santa Lucia he turned right again towards the Mission, right onto Rio Road to Highway One, and left to go over the hill to Monterey. I followed at a respectable distance.

In Monterey, my subject headed for the water. I was a block behind as he turned into the Fisherman's Wharf parking lot. I pulled in as he got out of the Camaro and walked towards Wharf Number Two.

His whole attitude was casual, as though he were a sightseer out for a pleasant stroll along the wharf. He would pause to watch a fishing boat unloading or a sea otter gliding along on its back, banging a shell between two rocks on its stomach.

At the end of the pier, my man was approached by a character in a Hollywood version of a seafaring costume who might have stepped out of *Moby Dick*. This self-consciously salty type was carrying what appeared to be a large picnic basket, which he handed over to Felicia's boy with a great yellow-toothed grin and a clap on the shoulder. The white-haired man winced perceptibly, accepted the basket, and gravely shook the hand of the hearty sailor.

I had to make a decision. The phony sailor had dumped his basket, delivered the goods. Couldn't do anything about him. I decided to follow the white-haired man and find out where the trail might end. I had a pretty good idea already.

I've got to say that I am really very good at surveillance. I've tailed some cagey ones; white-hair was one of them. But I managed this job quite well, indeed. My subject never picked up the tail— and I followed him all the way back to Felicia's house on Carmel Point.

19

"All but the blood. That doesn't fit."

IT WAS PRETTY obvious that the picnic basket did not contain fresh fish. Something was going on that just might be outside the law. Murder comes with complications. And the white-haired man looked pretty sneaky to me. But you can't arrest a man for sneakiness. If that were true, they'd have hauled away my high school math teacher.

Next morning, bright and early, much too early, Balestreri called. "I've got your picture, Riordan. Lab did a hell of a job. Same size as the original painting. Good color, too."

I had made arrangements to meet Reiko's uncle at the office to sign the lease and take care of some other paper work that morning.

"All right, Sergeant. Meet me as near noon as possible at the Village Corner in Carmel."

The Village Corner is an old Carmel landmark. In recent years it has been frequently threatened by developers who want to wipe out a whole block along Sixth and erect another shop complex. They've been able to grab two-thirds of the property. But the Corner has resisted and persisted, and is a pretty good place to eat, especially if you like Greek lemon soup. There's a pleasant patio and on this July day, warm for a change, I found a table in the corner at eleven forty-five.

I ordered coffee. The waitress gave me a hard look.

"I'm, uh, waiting for a friend. A policeman. We'll order when he gets here."

With a sidelong glance of disbelief and pure scorn, she moved away without speaking.

A few minutes before noon, Balestreri pushed his way through the gathering crowd, clutching a cardboard cylinder.

Although there was a cool breeze from the ocean, the sergeant's face was covered with a film of perspiration. For the first time since I had met him, Balestreri looked tired and harried.

"OK, Riordan, whatever it is, it had better be good. I am very wired today. This crazy murder is not enough. We got word from L.A. this morning. It's on the street that there's a very big drug connection that's been operating for several years in my county. Nobody knows who or where or what, but I'm supposed to run it down—because there was heroin in the corpse in this case."

He sat down heavily as nearby customers stared. The tourists come to Carmel expecting to see artists and writers and other strange beasts—but not an exasperated cop, sweating and complaining in a restaurant.

"Have a cup of coffee or an iced tea—a sandwich, maybe—relax. In a few minutes we'll walk quietly across the street and have a consultation about the picture I assume you have rolled up in that tube."

He muttered something that I couldn't make out and intimidated our truculent waitress into bringing him a well-done cheeseburger which he consumed in five bites. During this exercise, his eyes darted around the patio as if to spot one of the wanted criminals whose pictures decorated the wall of the sheriff's office. I told him about following the white-haired man. He gave no response.

I paid the check, and we jaywalked diagonally across Dolores to climb the stone steps of the Carmel Art Association, a cooperative enterprise for local painters and sculptors. It is my favorite place to browse. For one thing, I know most of the artists personally or by reputation. For another, I enjoy the company of the people who look after the place. They are charming, knowledgeable folk who always have a pleasant word or two. This time, however, I needed expert help. I was sure that the painting in Sheila Lord's cottage was not her work. I was equally sure that it was the work of a local artist. The technique was very familiar. I was *not* sure I wanted it identified.

Harris, the association manager, was in when we arrived, sitting in the office eating a brown-bag lunch. I outlined my problem to him while he wiped the salami grease and mayonnaise from his fingers. I unrolled the large photograph and thumb-tacked it to a piece of black mounting board, dragged a rickety wooden easel out of the storeroom, planted it in the middle of the main gallery, and arranged the light to bring out as much detail as possible. There was definitely no signature, not even an initial.

"The style is very familiar, though, lots of color, very loose," mused Harris.

"Oh, yes," he went on, "the style and the palette. Somebody we should know. There's the Yuan influence. But Yuan never used color that way. Maybe somebody in the crowd that painted with Yuan. Armand's not doing anything anymore. Maybe—Greg Farrell. Yes, the colors are more like Greg's."

I was afraid of that. It had crossed my mind the moment I saw the painting for the first time.

Harris frowned. "All but the blood. That doesn't fit. It's a different red, sort of rusty. Doesn't match any other red in the painting. Maybe if I could see the original...."

I glanced at my right index fingernail. I had scraped some paint from the painting. Did I still carry a trace of it? Or had it been washed away? I couldn't tell Balestreri anyhow. At least, not now.

"Is it Sheila?" I asked. "That hasn't been decided yet. What do you think?"

All of us stared intently at the face of the woman in the painting. It was indistinct, faintly smiling.

"The coloring is right," said Harris. "The hair is good—dark auburn. And the skin. Sheila was quite pale. Yes, I'd say so—I'd say it's Sheila from the color."

He shook his head slowly and frowned again. "But the face doesn't tell me anything. Greg did a lot of nudes like this...some of them don't look much like the model who posed for them. In the face, that is. This is a good painting—but the blood...depressing."

"Where do I find Farrell?" Balestreri's face was grim but he looked more composed than at lunch.

"I'll call him," I said, "and if he's home, we'll drive down. But you're probably wasting your time, Balestreri. I'd be willing to bet that Greg Farrell did not kill Sheila. He was a soldier...but he is a gentle man."

"Somebody probably said that about George Patton. Let's go, Riordan."

20

Balestreri and I didn't especially notice the scenery.

IN MY LEFT rear pants pocket, I carry a leather case that contains my driver's license, my credit cards, and a small piece of paper on which are inscribed about a dozen important telephone numbers. Aside from my own, I cannot—or will not—remember telephone numbers. As we walked back to the gallery office, I pulled the paper out of the case and checked my list for Greg Farrell.

As I dialed, I had the thought that if Greg happened to be painting in his studio, some distance up the narrow canyon from his house, he would never hear the phone. But we were lucky. A woman's voice answered, hesitantly.

"Hello?"

"Hello, is Greg around?" I asked, not at all surprised to have the phone answered by a female.

"He's painting. Up in his studio. I'm sorry, but it's quite a way up the hill, and I'm sure he couldn't hear me if I. . . ."

"Debbie?" I recognized the voice.

"Who is this?"

"Riordan. I was at your house."

There was a short silence.

"You'd like to know what I'm doing here, right?"

"Crossed my mind."

"Well, you've been curious about where I spend my time away

from home, Riordan. I guess you've got me. That's what George wanted, wasn't it?"

"I wasn't looking for you. I have a detective sergeant from the sheriff's office with me. He's very anxious to talk to Greg. We're on our way. If Greg comes down the hill, tell him to stay put. You, too. It'll take us maybe a half hour."

Her voice was small and resigned. "All right, Riordan." And she hung up.

Greg's place is about halfway to Big Sur, but just getting out of town might consume most of that half hour I mentioned. Once south of the river, it was smooth going. It's beautiful scenery— something people come thousands of miles for, and then drive too fast to see. To the ones who take their time, it all seems so familiar. The visitors have seen this stretch of the Pacific Coast so many times in television commercials, mostly for automobiles. A lot of them have a pretty good notion of it from watching the Crosby golf tournament on TV. And some even remember that long opening sequence in *Play Misty for Me* with Eastwood driving a little two-seater up the road in the dusk to get to his radio station. As a bona fide movie buff, I remember some awe-inspiring scenes that were background for Burton and Taylor in *The Sandpiper*. But that one always looked to me like the company maybe spent a week in Big Sur, and shot the rest of the beach scenes in Santa Monica.

Balestreri and I didn't especially notice the scenery. He was lost in some grim reverie, fingering the cardboard tube that contained our most important clue. I was looking forward to the pleasure of seeing Debbie Spelvin again.

It's easy to miss the driveway that takes you back to the hodge-podge of old wood that serves as shelter for Farrell and his guests. The place is actually two old shacks joined together. They've been here for nearly fifty years. Originally built to house prisoners who were working on the construction of the present coast road in the late thirties, they were occupied in recent years by some pretty colorful people, including a commune devoted to free love and cannabis.

Greg, who is resourceful and ingenious, has made the place very snug and homey. Not exactly the Mark Hopkins, mind you, but a shelter from the hostile world. There have been times in my apartment on Russian Hill that I have dreamed of living at Greg's place, especially around four in the morning on garbage day when the big truck's vibration shakes the building, and the sanitary engineers frisbee the lids back and forth.

Debbie was standing in the door when we drove up. In contrast to the charming and provocative costume she had worn when last we met, she wore faded blue jeans and a bulky navy sweater against the cool breeze which blew steadily from the ocean.

"He's still up there, Riordan."

"Fine, we'll all go up and see him. Mrs. Spelvin, this is Sergeant Balestreri. He's in charge of the investigation of Sheila's murder."

They both nodded soberly, and I pushed aside the high weeds that concealed the path that curved around the beehives before it climbed up the steep slope to the shack that Greg used as a studio. About halfway, I remembered it was quite a climb. No wonder Farrell could stay in such good shape. But I plunged on, trying to remember not to grab any of the poison oak for support.

Greg didn't seem surprised or disturbed to see us. He was working on a very large canvas, creating some sort of abstract, and he barely acknowledged our presence. His mind seemed to be in the middle distance, and his eyes focused on images we couldn't see.

"Hello," he said, smiling briefly at us, then at his palette, then at his painting.

I introduced Balestreri, and Greg gave the sergeant another warm, preoccupied smile. Debbie stood in the background quietly, eyes cast down.

After a moment of silence, the artist stepped back from his easel and announced: "It's finished. You arrived at precisely the right time. It's got all it needs. It's finished. Now...why are you here?"

I looked at the large abstract composition and said to myself, "How do they know? What makes it finished?"

Balestreri slid the photograph out of the tube and carefully unrolled it. He held it up for Greg to inspect. After a quick glance, Farrell turned to his just-completed canvas and gently lifted it from the easel. Placing the new painting against the wall, he selected an unused canvas from a stack nearby and adjusted it on the easel. He arranged the photograph against it, overlapping slightly at the top and bottom, and clamped it securely.

"There, that's better. Not a bad painting. Not mine. Looks like mine, but it's not. Sloppy job with the blood. Don't like that color at all. Doesn't look like blood."

He was calm, matter-of-fact. He appraised the painting coolly and professionally. "Too bad I can't see the original. I painted...oh, seven or eight like this. Same model. Seated nude, reclining nude. Sold a couple of them at a gallery in Menlo Park. There are others still here."

He darted across the room to a stack of unframed paintings and rummaged through them until he found what he was looking for. "Here's one," he said with a grin of triumph. He held up a painting of a female nude in a languorous pose on a chaise longue, her eyes half-closed, a gentle smile on her lips. It came within millimeters of being the twin of our photograph. Except, of course, that there was no blood—and the hair on the model was jet black.

21

"Think what my paintings will be worth if I make it to the gas chamber!"

BALESTRERI EVENTUALLY got around to asking the customary murder suspect questions.

On the night of the murder, Greg declared, he had been at home through the evening, reading a new novel by John Updike. ("Guy's got a big thing about pubic hair.") He had retired at about ten-thirty and slept through to six-thirty—just about the time that Marie woke me and led me to the body of Sheila Lord.

"Can anybody back you up?" asked the sergeant.

"Debbie called me about nine. We talked for maybe fifteen minutes. Does that count?"

"It's only one board in what ought to be a big fence. Especially since I hear you and Mrs. Spelvin are pretty good friends."

That Balestreri. He doesn't miss a trick. He had picked up on the relationship between Greg and Debbie somewhere.

"Sure, we're good friends." Greg flashed an engaging smile. "She's in my oils class."

The lady, who had remained silent since Balestreri and I had arrived, finally looked at me and said: "Did you talk to Sheila's Aunt Felicia?"

Greg's smile vanished. "Felicia!" He bit the word off viciously. "I had almost forgotten about that evil old woman. Yes, Felicia . . . ."

Farrell's whole aspect had changed. The mention of Miss

Montalvo's name struck a disagreeable chord within him that altered his attitude and his appearance. There was none of the happy-go-lucky artist about him when he spoke: "Let me tell you about Aunt Felicia. That mean old bitch has more money than all the people in the Del Monte Forest put together. And you know how she got it? Gambling, porno movies, dirty books, call girls, drugs—you name it. She had a piece of just about any kind of action from San Francisco to Santa Barbara. She is the toughest, wickedest old woman in the eleven western states, and she passes herself off as some kind of nobility in that big house on the Point."

He paused and his expression softened. He glanced at Debbie. She quickly looked away.

"I had an affair with Sheila, if that's what you want to call it. You could even say that I loved her in my fashion. But Felicia found out and, for her own reasons, violently disapproved. She sent her white-haired soldier around to see me. He made it plain that if I didn't stay clear of Sheila, he would cause me great bodily harm. And from what Sheila had told me, I knew he could do it. He had been some sort of Nevada enforcer before Felicia had picked him up as what you might call a combination administrative assistant and body-guard."

I glanced at Balestreri. He was nodding. He already knew about Felicia's handyman.

Greg went on: "You know what they say about discretion, and I am nothing if not discreet. I told Sheila we had better call it off for the sake of my health and maybe hers. This was back in February. She took it pretty hard. Went a little crazy. That's when she almost set the Ranch on fire one Saturday night with the bonfire made of all her paintings and painting materials. I felt pretty bad about it. But I never saw her after that—except at a distance. I couldn't have made her pregnant.

"I'm sorry, Pat, that I played so dumb when you first asked me about Sheila. Knowing what people were saying about Sheila and me—I guess I was afraid I'd be dragged into this mess and even suspected of murder."

His smile reappeared suddenly. "Think what my paintings will be worth if I make it to the gas chamber!"

Nobody laughed. Debbie, who had returned to her nervous, red-eyed silence, walked deliberately out the door and started down the path. Greg shrugged and followed her, clutching a handful of brushes. Balestreri and I trailed them down the hill.

Farrell paused at the door of his house. "You going to arrest me?"

Balestreri shook his head briskly. "Not now, my friend. You may be innocent. You may be a liar and a cold-blooded murderer. Right now, I don't know. But don't leave the area, understand?"

We allowed Debbie to wheel her red Ferrari out on the narrow drive and north on Highway One towards Carmel. I settled my car about fifty yards behind her at a comfortable speed. The fog was beginning to drift in with the freshening breeze. Streaks and patches of the gray mist floated by and stretched up into the creases of the hills to our right.

"I cannot bring myself to believe that man is telling the whole truth, Riordan. He admitted he lied to you about his relationship with Sheila Lord."

The sergeant had dropped his seat back a couple of notches and was resting comfortably with his eyes closed. He tapped his forehead with the cardboard tube.

"Your friend Mrs. Spelvin has more to tell us, also. Why was she there, anyhow? If she were just a student, you'd think she'd be up watching the guy paint. But here she is at his house, maybe brewing up a pot of tea."

Balestreri opened his eyes a little and rolled them toward me. He knew as well as I what was going on—or what had been going on—between Debbie and Greg.

"You got the hots for the blonde lady, Riordan? I saw you looking at her. Better watch it. She's a dazzler. You and Farrell are supposed to be friends."

He gave me a wicked leer. Balestreri's persona was constantly shifting from sophisticated detective to macho cop and back again. He closed his eyes and settled back. He seemed to be talking to himself. "And Farrell really hates the old lady, the aunt. That ought to be the next step. I knew about her white-haired boy. He brought a reputation with him, and we've been watching him ever since he came into the county. But we figured he was just working for a rich old lady who needed protection. We didn't make the connection until recently. She's really in the rackets all right. How come Farrell knew that before we did? Shit!"

He seemed to doze the rest of the way into the village, so I left him alone. It didn't seem to bother him when I flipped on the radio and listened to all the other bad news of the day.

22

"I need to be free of the guilt, Mr. Riordan."

There's this man who's been trying to get you all day, Riordan. He's called every half hour since about nine-thirty, but he won't leave a name or a number."

Reiko was bringing me up to date on what had gone on in the office during my absence. In the short time we've been here, she has organized us beyond belief and, when I was out of the office, was lending her expertise to everybody else in the building. Perhaps one day she will write a book on office efficiency (or create "software," the ultimate organizer). She will leave me then, and I will go back to cryptic notes on scraps of paper.

"Voice wasn't familiar?"

"Not to me. Maybe a trace of an accent. Nobody I've talked to before, I'd swear it."

"He'll call again."

Reiko disentangled her legs from her Norwegian backless chair and perched on the edge of her desk. "What do you think happened to Nancy's father, Harding Blanchard, Pat? Why has no trace of him ever been found? Do you think he's still alive?"

"A lot of people succeed in disappearing, honey. If they really want to. It's not that hard if you're reasonably intelligent. It's not as if Blanchard were a criminal on the run. He's probably just a guy who busted out of an unhappy marriage and found joy driving a cab in Honolulu."

Reiko rocked back and forth, shaking her head. "I don't think so. I don't think so."

I went into my office and looked through the mail. Some bills and lots of junk.

The phone rang. I heard Reiko answer. In a moment she called through the partition: "It's him, Riordan."

I got on the line. "Hello, this is Riordan."

"Mr. Riordan, you will remember me. Raul Jimenez?"

Raul, could I ever forget you? Nancy Blanchard's first major fling. Adele could have had you put away for statutory rape, but instead she used her considerable influence to keep the whole distasteful mess out of the papers, and by the time the police heard about the affair from one of those ever-present little birds, you were gone, long gone.

"Raul, you're the one guy I thought I'd never hear from again."

"Mr. Riordan, I need to talk to you. It is very important. But it must be very private."

His voice was urgent.

"What's it all about, Raul?"

"I cannot tell you on the telephone, Mr. Riordan."

"OK, we'll talk. How about Monastery Beach? There'll be some scuba divers down there, but they won't notice us. I can be there in twenty minutes."

"Very well, Mr. Riordan. I am quite near there now. I will watch for you."

I'd thought I was free of the Blanchard case when Nancy grew up and went out on her own. Now here was Raul, who went back a good eight years.

It's tough enough to make a living in my business without giving your time away. George would pay me. And Adele Blanchard would, too. But I didn't stand to make a dime from the Sheila Lord affair. And now, Raul had come out of the past, probably without a buck or a credit card.

He was waiting for me at the edge of the road at Monastery Beach. The wind off the ocean was bitter and cold, so I invited him into the car.

Raul was pretty much as I remembered him. Slender build,

well-muscled, hair jet black, face unlined. Quite a handsome man. More mature, perhaps not quite the threatening Latin lover type he had seemed to be when I found him with Nancy in a Modesto motel.

"I have been away, Mr. Riordan, for a long while. I left in a hurry, as you know. And I have been afraid. Now I want to come back. My children are grown, and I need to see them. My wife has forgiven me and will take me once more to her heart."

Raul spoke softly and his eyes never met mine. "I wrote to Mrs. Blanchard asking for help. But she will not give me the help I need, only money. She is without feeling, that woman."

He wrote to Adele? What a strange thing to do.

"I need to be free of the guilt, Mr. Riordan. I am guilty of violating a young girl. I have hidden myself in many bad places all these years, I have worked at bad jobs. Mrs. Blanchard sent me money, but I sent it all to my wife. I worked in the fields. But now I want to go home."

I felt like telling him that he hadn't been the first to "violate" Nancy. But the man was so contrite, so helpless.

"Why did you call me? How did you find me?"

"When I came back to Carmel, I looked in the phone directory. I found Nancy. When I called her, she gave me your number. I remembered that you were a good man."

"What can this good man do for you, Raul?"

"Perhaps—perhaps you can help me make the deal. With the police. You see, I know something that is known by very few. Something that is evil. It is the reason why Mrs. Blanchard allowed me to disappear eight years ago, the reason she has sent me money."

"You're going to have to tell me about it, Raul."

Raul breathed deeply and, after a long pause, began his story: "Mr. Blanchard, Nancy's father, was a very nice man. Mrs. Blanchard treated him like dirt. She owned him—like she owned the house and the yacht and the Bugatti. He needed love, so he took up with many women who were below his station."

Raul paused and took another deep breath. "He would even bring the women home with him when his wife and daughter were away. And they took many trips together. But one time they returned earlier than expected. The two of them, Nancy and Mrs. Blanchard, found Mr. Blanchard and this young girl naked in his bed. Before the eyes of his daughter and his wife, he took a pistol from the drawer in his bedside table, put the barrel in his mouth—and blew out his brains."

My vision of Harding Blanchard leading the good life as a cab driver in the Islands disappeared in a flash.

"I learned of these things from the girl. She was a cocktail waitress in Carmel, and she told me that Nancy had fainted when her father took his life, but Mrs. Blanchard ignored her daughter lying at her feet and watched as the girl dressed and left the house. She left town soon after these things happened, driving a new, expensive automobile."

Raul looked out at the beach, where three scuba divers were shedding their tanks and peeling off their wet suits.

"We buried him, Mrs. Blanchard and I, between two liveoak trees behind the house. I burned the bloody sheets and pillow cases and cleaned the mess in Mr. Blanchard's bedroom. She swore me to absolute silence."

He looked back at me.

"And then I was a fool. Then I began the affair with Nancy. And you know the rest."

23

"Want to go fishing?"

I DROPPED RAUL off at a little shack in an artichoke field with a warning to keep out of sight for a few days until I could get a handle on the situation.

The most significant element in Raul's whole story was the traumatic effect that witnessing her father's suicide must have had on Nancy Blanchard. Her blackout on the night of Sheila Lord's murder and the subsequent fear that she might have killed Sheila could be related to that terrible shock and might have nothing to do with this case. I made a mental note to talk to Nancy and her San Francisco psychiatrist.

Adele would be something else. I had no doubt about her motive for burying her husband and pretending he had disappeared. A suicide in the family meant a severe loss of face. At least, to Adele. It also explained why she had sold the Pebble Beach house and moved into the condo in High Meadow.

I went home. It was one of those nights when living alone was painful. I opened a can of minestrone and a box of crackers. I snapped on the TV and watched an incredibly dumb show in which five thousand rounds of ammunition were fired and nobody was hit.

About ten o'clock, the phone rang.

"Riordan?" It was Balestreri's voice.

"Yeah, Sergeant, what's up?"

"Remember I told you about the dope thing in the county? Heroin coming in?"

"Sure."

"Want to go fishing?"

I was curious. Balestreri had been warming up a little since our first encounter, but I didn't expect a social invitation.

"Are you serious?"

"You bet, Riordan. Listen, I've been nosing around since we found out that Sheila Lord was full of dope when she died. Guess whose name keeps coming up from the street? The old broad, the aunt, Felicia Montalvo."

This was not an astonishing revelation.

"The operation has been going on for a long time. The dope comes out of Mexico. Hell, they used to swim it up the coast to San Diego. They had young kids who'd strap loads of dope on their backs in Tijuana and pop up on isolated beaches in California. You know what the markups are on heroin as it goes through channels to the street. The kids would load up with the pure stuff and swim it in, couple o' hundred thousand bucks worth at a time."

He seemed pleased.

"Anyway, the people down south got that pretty well shut off, but meanwhile the dealers had gotten the idea of sending the stuff out in little pleasure boats, even sailboats. At first they landed in San Pedro, where there are a lot of marinas. When the pressure got too bad there, they moved farther up the coast: Santa Barbara, Pismo Beach. Now it's coming in here, scattered around in small craft. There's damn little commerce in Monterey Harbor, except for the fishing boats.

"And you know who controls the traffic in almost anything illegal in Monterey County? Felicia Montalvo, the aristocratic lady with the big nose who lives in that expensive house on the Point and paints other people's pictures."

What was it Felicia had said to me? "I am in semi-retirement from several lucrative businesses."

I told Balestreri I'd meet him on the Monterey waterfront the next day.

Monterey has two "Fisherman's Wharves," referred to simply as

Number One and Number Two. Number One is for tourists: restaurants, souvenir shops, sightseeing boats. You eat fish and feed the sea lions. Number Two is strictly utilitarian. Between them lies a marina of mixed breeds of craft, from rusty commercial fishing boats to slick private yachts.

In good weather, the small craft move in and out of the marina freely. Visitors can drop anchor in the shallows north of Wharf Number two. It's possible to unload small quantities of any kind of cargo almost anywhere.

Many of the commercial fishing boats are now run by Vietnamese. These are refugees who know no other way of making a living. And there's a lot of resentment among the old Italian and Portuguese families who have been fishing Monterey Bay for generations, but nothing so serious that it might hamper the operation of anyone whose business it is simply to deliver drugs.

Balestreri and I hung around the end of Wharf Number Two for nearly an hour. I didn't know what we were waiting for and didn't ask. Presently we were approached by a thin, blond young man wearing rimless glasses and an almost invisible mustache.

"Riordan, this is Al McManus. He's federal narcotics. This is mainly their case. Tell him what you saw the other day."

I told the federal agent about following Felicia's man and witnessing the passing of the picnic basket.

"What did he look like?" McManus asked.

"Hard to tell. He was got up to look real salty—like Spencer Tracy in *Captains Courageous*. But I'd bet the color came from number ten pancake and the clothes from a costume rental outfit."

McManus, who looked nervous and uncomfortable, found it difficult to stand still. He would shift his feet constantly, moving only a few inches in any direction.

"See anybody here that looks like the guy with the basket?"

There weren't many choices at that moment, and they all looked like the real thing: men involved in a construction project at the end of the wharf, commercial fishermen, two tourists in loud shirts and ill-fitting polyester slacks.

"Nope. I strongly suspect that our guy only gets into his seafaring outfit to make deliveries—and he could be anywhere right now."

"Do you think you could recognize him out of make-up?"

I thought about it. The man had worn one of those Greek caps, and the hair under it looked like a wig. But his face was clean-shaven. Actor's ego, I guess: nothing in the way of the face, which was no doubt full of character. Yeah, I remember now. Great eyebrows, heavy and dark. A prominent but well-shaped nose. And a mouthful of big yellow teeth. He was under six feet, but taller than Felicia's errand boy, and in his late forties, maybe early fifties.

I told all this to McManus.

"I could probably spot him. His walk was funny, though. An actor, giving his impression of a sailor."

"Keep your eyes open, Riordan. Call me if anything comes up. So long, Tony."

McManus pressed his card into my hand and shook hands with Balestreri. Eyes darting in all directions, he walked briskly away.

24

"Ah, well, c'est la vie."

A CALL TO Nancy Blanchard's psychiatrist in San Francisco got me nothing but the usual medical evasiveness and gobbledegook. The man was courteous and probably competent, but unwilling to discuss the case beyond the fact that the girl was seriously disturbed. After a few minutes, I figured the call wasn't worth the message units, thanked the doctor, and hung up.

Nancy had a date to go to a concert with Sheila Lord on the night of Sheila's murder. Nancy left the house to pick Sheila up. Nancy can't remember anything until late the following morning when she woke up after a nightmare in which she saw Sheila dead.

About the only concrete thing Nancy's doctor had been willing to tell me was that he had prescribed a "fairly strong" tranquilizing drug, and also a "mood elevator." I'm not an expert, but I've always been suspicious of chemicals that mess with people's heads, legally or not.

About all I could do at this point was confront Adele Blanchard with the whole bloody mess: Nancy's fears and problems, as well as the bizarre tale told by Raul.

I drove up to High Meadow. On that day the expensive homes and condos stood in bright sunshine above the fog that swirled through Carmel, Pebble Beach, and Pacific Grove. High Meadow has a sort of Olympian feeling. I suspect that's why Adele chose to settle there.

Adele opened the door in response to my ring. She looked exactly as she had looked to me in the years that I had known her: blue hair, flat shoes, monumental presence.

She also looked nervous and puzzled.

"Mr. Riordan, won't you come in?"

She ushered me down a hall into a large high-ceilinged living room. She indicated a chair for me and arranged herself artfully on a couch.

"May I offer you tea? I keep hot water on all the time. I do have instant coffee, although I think it's vile stuff."

The usual amenities. Adele knew I was there for a purpose and I knew she knew. But this little ritual had to come first.

"No thanks to the tea...or the coffee. Nancy thinks she might have killed Sheila Lord. What do you think?"

The face did not change but there was a long silence.

"That is impossible, Mr. Riordan. I know that Nancy and Sheila were planning to go to the concert that night. But...."

She shuddered. Until that moment I had never seen Adele at a loss for words, or the least bit out of control. But it seemed that she somehow knew that deep and shameful secrets were about to burst out into the open.

"I...I've been having Nancy followed. A local man, adequate but unimaginative. He lost her completely when she ran off to San Francisco, and I called...you."

She leaned forward to make a slight adjustment to a flower arrangement on the coffee table. "There is a complete report on the night in question, of course, and a witness. Nancy went to Sheila's cottage and knocked on the door. There was no answer. She knocked again and again with no response. She went to the concert alone.

"My man followed her from the theatre to Sheila's cottage again after the concert. This time she tried the door and found it open. She went inside for a matter of seconds and came stumbling out, as the detective described it, making strange sounds. She got in her car and drove back to her own place and, as my man had it, apparently retired for the night."

Adele was composed now. "I have no doubt that she was severely traumatized by what she saw in Sheila's cottage, and no doubt that she went home and took a handful of pills from that expensive San Francisco doctor. Poor thing can't even remember the concert."

"You know about the doctor, then?"

"Mr. Riordan, I have paid that man's excessive bills for years, ever since. . . ."

She went blank. She had gone farther than she wanted to. I saw on her face an expression that might have been on Marie Antoinette's as she was expecting the blade to drop.

"Raul's back, Mrs. Blanchard."

That was the blade. Her face collapsed, her body seemed to shrink.

"He told me why you didn't insist that he be prosecuted, why you sent him money, how your husband died, and how you and he buried Harding Blanchard's body.

"And he told me that Nancy witnessed her father's suicide and fell into a faint. It was then that you began sending her to the psychiatrist, wasn't it, Mrs. Blanchard?"

Adele got up, walked to a sideboard, and poured half a snifter of brandy from a crystal decanter.

"Mr. Riordan, I have always been able to arrange things, to dictate, to control. But I suppose I knew my luck would run out one day. Ah, well, *c'est la vie.*"

And she downed the brandy in one smooth swallow.

25

"He told me—I was a nice lady."

THE SUN takes a long time to go down on the Pacific Coast.

I drove down from High Meadow directly into the glare of the setting sun, and realized that it was July and Daylight Saving Time, and it must be close to eight o'clock.

When I got to the house I called Reiko at her apartment.

"Where've you been? I've been calling your place since five. You've got to let me know what's going on. How the hell am I going to be able to help you if you don't let me know what's going on?"

She was angry and her voice had an edge on it. "How's your head? Have you had anything to eat? You ought to get some exercise, too, run on the beach or something."

Meekly, I told her about my visit to Adele. She listened patiently to my story, punctuating it with little "ahs" and "ohs."

At length, she seemed satisfied and, with the command that I go have dinner, she hung up.

At that moment, I realized how much she meant to me. There is something between us that would never make one of Barbara Cartland's novels. But it will last as long as we last.

Reiko was right about one thing: I hadn't eaten. I walked down the hill to an Italian place and had a plate of fettucine al pesto, heavy with garlic. I figured I'd be sleeping alone.

The phone was ringing when I got back to the house. I glanced at my watch as I picked it up. Nine-thirty or thereabouts. I can't see my watch very clearly without my drugstore reading glasses.

"Hello."

"Riordan. This is—Debbie Spelvin. I'm sorry to bother you but —I mean, this is sort of stupid—could I see you tonight? Not here. George is here. He's drunk, but he's here. I had the number of your house. I know what George used to use it for. I can be there in ten minutes—if it's all right."

Normally, I am in full control of my emotions. I've had a lot of errant wives offer to go to bed with me if I'd just phony up the report. But this was another kind of woman. I felt a slow flush creep up the back of my neck.

"Sure. Come on over. Bring your own booze."

She was right about the time. Just a shade over ten minutes.

She had changed her image completely since I had last seen her in an oversized sweater and jeans. She was a vision of stunning elegance in a navy blazer over a cream-colored blouse and a skirt whose color I would never attempt to name. Helen, whose career was wrapped up in *haute couture*, used to chide me for my ignorance. To me, colors were all variations of the primary— everything was some kind of red, orange, yellow, green, blue, or violet. So I don't talk about color in the presence of women.

Debbie brought with her the scent of perfume that I remembered so well from our first meeting. She sat down and crossed her legs the way my mother had told me a lady should cross her legs.

"The crack about bringing my own booze, Riordan. That was unnecessary."

"I'm sorry. You took me by surprise."

"I guess I did. I guess I've got some explaining to do."

I stood rather awkwardly in front of the fireplace and waited. This was the wife of the man who employed me. I was just a bit flushed, and there was no fire in the fireplace.

"Riordan, I've told you some of my story. Innocent little girl from broken home in Chicago ends up wife of Pebble Beach millionaire. It's all true. But...I want you to understand. I think you're a good guy, Riordan. You're a throwback of some sort. I didn't know what to make of you at first. But I'm sure now that you're a good guy. An old-fashioned good guy."

She uncrossed her legs and crossed them the other way, and I had a couple of pre-ventricular contractions.

"I went down to Greg's place that day to make damn sure that the messages I had been getting from him were for real. I don't mean little pieces of paper. I mean little looks and moves that were telling me to back off.

"Greg is all up-front, Riordan. He told me in so many words that I was a nice lady...but no thanks. He didn't mean to...but he made me feel ashamed.

"I don't know why I came on so strong with Greg. Suddenly it was so important to me to be loved. All my life I had been falling in love with really rotten men. I saw myself as I am. Married for money to a nice old drunk who never hurt anybody.

"I look in the mirror now, Riordan, and see it all going away. I'll be forty-four in October. I told George I was ten years younger. But the mirror said it, Riordan. It's all going away."

There were tears in her eyes as she raised them to mine. She seemed no less beautiful to me than she had seemed a minute before.

"You understand, don't you? I married George for his money, yes, but also to avoid getting old alone. I was unfair to George and unfair to myself.

"I tried to settle in and be Mrs. Spelvin of Pebble Beach. But George wasn't about to change his habits. After a couple of months of a pleasant honeymoon, he just wandered off and picked up his old saloon schedule. It was what he had always done. And usually the new bride would begin quiet talks with a lawyer. After a while there'd be a generous settlement, and George would get into the pattern again."

Of course she wasn't telling me anything I didn't already know. I had been part of the pattern.

"I made it clear to George that he was not going to pay me off and send me away. That seemed to shake him up. It also made me more interesting to him. It was a new experience. He turned possessive and suspicious.

"When I told you that I was not cruising the bars looking to get laid, it was the truth. I've never gone in for one-night stands. I was strongly attracted to Armand Colbert. He's charming and very European. I still think he's one of the most attractive men I know.

"But Greg—Greg is the dream of my youth: a free spirit, gentle and kind. I was foolish over Greg. That ended when you saw me at his place. He told me—I was a nice lady."

She rose from her chair and came very close to me. She threw back her head and engaged me with those wide green eyes. At that moment, I realized that I was absolutely enchanted by this woman. I reached out and touched her face.

"I never went to bed with Armand or Greg. I knew you'd understand, Riordan. You *must* understand."

I don't think I believed her then, nor do I now. But what the hell. She took both of my hands in hers, and the scent of her perfume was intoxicating.

I don't remember who made the first move, but it really doesn't matter. I was kissing her, and her mouth was hot and moving. I pulled her close to me, and her hand was like fire as it slid under my shirt. An all-consuming desire came over me as I led her slowly up the narrow stairs.

26

Suddenly, in the warmth of the house, a chill took me.

IT WAS STILL dark when the phone woke me. Debbie was gone.

"Riordan?" Balestreri didn't wait for me to say hello.

"Yeah."

"Well, the aunt is out of it, Riordan. There'll be no more information from her. There was damn little anyhow. They found her about a half hour ago on the rocks at the north end of Carmel River Beach, with her head smashed. And she hadn't been dead very long. I'm in Pacific Grove, but I'll be on the scene in about fifteen minutes. Meet me there."

I was at a point where I didn't give a damn about Felicia Montalvo or George Spelvin or even Sheila Lord's killer. It is not appropriate that an intelligent man in middle age should burn with adolescent passion for a lady in middle age. But the scent of her perfume was still on me, and the imprint of her body on the bed beside me.

I crawled out of bed and hit the shower, hoping that the cold water that always arrives a couple of minutes before the hot water would jolt me out of the vague melancholy that I felt. Dressing was going through the motions. I just picked up anything that was handy, some of it from the floor.

The spot where Felicia Montalvo died was not far from my house, and I could get over there in maybe five minutes. The wind was strong that morning and carried a chill with it. I pulled on a lined, hooded green jacket and ducked out into the dark dawn. It was just after four-thirty.

Carmel River Beach is at the end of Carmelo Street where it meets Scenic Road. It's a place the tourists seldom discover. There are always plenty of wet-suited scuba divers in good weather. And when it's really warm, the beach gets pretty thick with people. But the strangers who pass through town from Iowa, Pennsylvania, and British Columbia don't often find it.

At the northernmost edge of the beach, just under the point where Scenic Drive makes a blind right-angle turn, is a granite outcropping that extends out into the water. Balestreri had arrived only a minute or so before I did, and I found him, bundled in a yellow all-weather coat and a black knit cap, standing over the body of Felicia Montalvo.

The old woman lay on her back as if she were sunbathing on the rocks, her black eyes wide open and a look of astonishment on her face. The back of her head was just red mush.

Balestreri nodded as I approached. "Some kids found her," he said. "They were sleeping on the beach and the guy got up to pee. The way we figure, so far, is that she fell from up there." He pointed up the hill to the ninety-degree corner of Scenic directly above.

A vaguely familiar voice came from behind me. "You like blood and guts, detective? You make a hobby of being at murder scenes? You know this guy, Tony?" It was Marshall from the coroner's office.

I gave him a sweet smile. "Just lucky, I guess, Doctor. What have you made of this one? Foul play?"

"Well, she came off the road up there, I think. It's a fair guess at this point that her head was smashed on this rock, and not by a blunt instrument. It's hard to tell, anyhow. There's more, though. If she had just fallen, she'd most probably have rolled a ways and been broken up some. There's no real sharp drop. I made a quick check of the body. Bad contusions on the left side and hip, and a couple of broken ribs. It's only a guess at this point, but as I make it, she was walking around the turn on the outside and a car got her."

Balestreri showed some interest. "Hit and run?" he asked.

"Or something deliberate. Who knows? If it was planned, it had to be planned very well. The old lady had to be bounced far enough so she'd land on the rocks. Oh, hell, I don't know. All that's plain is that she was bumped off the road and fell down here and smashed her head. I'll take her down to the morgue and see if I can find anything else."

I shivered in the cold foggy wind. A pretty good surf was up, and the salt spray was wetting my hair and stinging my eyes. I thought about the July tourist in his T-shirt and shorts, bitching about the California summer cold.

Balestreri looked very tired—a hard-working, compassionate policeman who sometimes hated his job; not really the bristling, intimidating cop I first took him to be. We stood in silence as the gentle-handed men from the coroner's office bagged the body and took it across the sand.

"The next step," Balestreri said through his teeth, "the next step is to go to the lady's house and see if anything presents itself." I agreed, smiling to myself despite the cold and gloom and the presence of death. I was teamed up with Hercule Poirot.

We walked back to the parking lot and got into Balestreri's car. The Montalvo house was not far away. It looked pleasantly inviting as we drove up. Warm light radiated from the studio's glass wall.

As I was about to knock, Balestreri put his hand on my arm. Silently, he reached out with two fingers and tapped the door, which swung slowly open. The sergeant stepped forward and entered the hallway. I followed. Inside, we both paused and listened.

"Anybody here?" Balestreri called out.

No sound. Just the surf a couple of blocks away.

Together we walked through the ground floor rooms. Everything was in order. The house was decorated in excellent taste and the rooms were warm and comfortable. But everything had the wax-works look of sample rooms in a high-class furniture store. The kitchen looked like one of the food labs at *Sunset* Magazine.

We found nothing unusual in our search, not even a butt in one of the beautiful ceramic ashtrays. The only thing out of the ordinary was the overwhelming presence of art.

There were paintings everywhere, in every room. The two walls of the kitchen not taken up with cabinets and appliances were covered with paintings. In the other rooms, all four walls were broken into rectangles of varying sizes from a line about thirty inches from the floor.

No style of oil painting was omitted. Piet Mondrian hung beside Degas, Jackson Pollack was a neighbor of Andrew Wyeth. And all of them—I knew—fakes.

Suddenly, in the warmth of the house, a chill took me. I motioned Balestreri to follow me into the dining room. We had been in it moments before, checking closets and pulling open drawers. But something had registered in my subconscious. I hadn't been looking for it, and I must have looked right through it.

In the middle of a wall, just slightly askew, was an oil painting of a nude in a languorous pose on a chaise longue. Her hair was auburn and her flesh was pale and there was an inviting smile on her face. There wasn't a drop of blood on her.

27

"A drunken asshole truck driver..."

Is THAT it, Riordan?"

"Very little question. But who knows how many of these things there are—pretty much alike to the untrained eye. Like all those banal seascapes in the gallery windows."

"Somebody cleaned up the blood," mused Balestreri. "Can that be done, Riordan? I mean, without messing up the rest of the painting?"

"Sure, there are ways. No real problem. It all depends...." I stopped.

When I walked into the living room of Sheila Lord's cottage that morning, the painting was wet. I touched it with my finger and wiped my finger on the floor. Oils can take a long time to dry.

"Sergeant, was the painting dry when your people put it back on the easel before you left Lord's place?"

"I don't know. Looked plenty dry. One of our guys picked it up, and I told him to stand up the easel and put it back. The photographer came over and took a couple of shots. Sure, it had to be dry."

At that moment, I felt that I had a real piece of the puzzle in my hand. All I had to do was find the odd-shaped gap in the picture that it would fit. There were still a lot of pieces that were all blue sky.

Balestreri and I became simultaneously aware of a rustling sound and quiet footsteps above us. The sergeant made a sound in his throat and bounded out into the hall and up the narrow staircase. I followed as closely as I could without stepping on his heels. We had both forgotten the studio, from which all these brazenly unoriginal paintings flowed.

The scene we came upon was strange and oddly beautiful. The studio was lighted expertly and expensively. The whole room was suffused with what could have been mistaken for muted daylight.

Seated in the middle of the floor on a tatami mat, in the shadow of Felicia's great easel, was the white-haired man, the old lady's errand boy and guardian. He wore a black turtleneck, and his legs were folded in the full lotus.

The man raised his face as we entered. Again, it struck me as strange that in the deeply tanned face the eyes were a clear turquoise blue. Those eyes were calm, but glistening with a hint of tears, and the man's face signalled pain.

"I know she is dead, gentlemen. I saw her killed."

He nodded slowly and inclined his head toward the floor. He continued to speak: "She did not sleep well. She would rise in the night at any hour and walk. From here along the Scenic Drive to the foot of Ocean and back again. It was my job to accompany her. I was not companion to her thoughts. I followed at ten paces."

He breathed deeply and paused. "We were returning this morning, the fog was patchy and blowing steadily from the sea. She was ahead of me, approaching the blind turn overlooking the beach. From behind us at a reckless speed came a pickup truck. A massive dog barked at me from the cab's right window. I heard the sound of the vehicle's brakes and in the dimness saw the pickup fishtail through the turn, tilting sharply as the left front wheel left the road momentarily. It recovered miraculously and continued down the hill, gaining speed. A drunken driver, gentlemen. A drunken asshole truck driver...."

For some reason, the word "asshole" sounded ridiculous in the rather over-precise speech of Felicia Montalvo's hired hand. He stopped, closed his eyes, and drew another long breath.

"Felicia simply disappeared. I ran to the edge of the bluff and saw her body on the rocks. When I climbed down to her, I saw immediately that she was dead. Her head was crushed. She was over seventy, gentlemen, and she had led a life fraught with danger. And she was killed by a drunken bastard in a pickup truck because she was an insomniac.

"She is gone and they will kill me soon. Without her protection, I will be killed. It's inevitable. The people from Nevada. They will kill me."

The inevitable conclusion. Chinese restaurants never serve breakfast.

The man had been talking in a soft monotone, eyes cast down. He looked up, an expression of utter resignation in his face. I had noticed during his long speech that he had an accent of some sort, British or Australian.

Balestreri stood silent a moment. He wanted to ask questions but the exotic quality of the scene had slowed him down. He couldn't think what to ask first.

"Who are you?" was the best he could do—although I knew he already had a full background on the man.

"My name is Eric Farnham." The monotone continued: "I was born in the village of Malvern Wells, Worcestershire, in 1937. I have been in this country just over thirty years, and I am a naturalized citizen. Is that what you want? Or do you really want to know about my relationship with Miss Montalvo and why I will be killed?"

"I want to know everything about you and Montalvo and what happened to Sheila Lord. And about that picture downstairs." Balestereri was businesslike again, taking charge.

The white-haired man sighed. "One thing at a time," he said.

Farnham's story began, of course, with his Las Vegas connection. He had traveled California and the northwest for a syndicate of owners of small clubs in the semi-official capacity of collector. He was authorized by his employers to use whatever methods he chose to collect money owed to them. For his efforts, he was paid a retainer and a small percentage. His mistake had been to underestimate the intelligence of the club owners. They were men who practiced the fine old Nevada principle: "The edge is always with the house, or it better damn well be." Farnham should have known. It was a stupid mistake for an old pro. There's always somebody watching the guy who is watching the pit boss who is watching the dealer.

Farnham had juggled his books on collections and skimmed off the top. His employers had eventually discovered his practice and hired another agency to eliminate him.

Through mutual friends, he had met Felicia Montalvo in San Jose, and he fled to her when he realized that there was a contract out on him. Needing a companion and bodyguard, she had taken him in with the stern warning to keep clean. She had called in a few favors to get the Nevada boys to pull off their hit men.

"Nobody would trifle with Felicia in her own territory. The Nevada people agreed to cancel the hit—at least temporarily—and I was safe as long as I remained in Montalvo's employ. The timing was especially propitious. I had grown up by the sea and knew the ways of the waterfront."

Balestreri and I looked at each other. This was the man's chief value to Felicia Montalvo. He was her traffic director for the drug flow through Monterey Harbor. And with her death, he was himself a sitting duck.

28

"Not especially bright. Often artists aren't."

I'M SORRY, gentlemen," said the white-haired man. "I guess I'm getting a bit ahead of myself.

"Felicia Montalvo was not just my protector and employer. I regarded her as a kind of genius. Or perhaps she just had a gift for seeing clearly the simple, obvious things."

Montalvo, he told us, had devised the scheme for bringing in drugs by small boat through the port of Monterey. She reasoned, rightly, that there would be far less danger there than at other ports along the coast. I could bear witness to the fact that the delivery of the goods was almost too simple to be believed. I remembered the phony sailor who could have come off any one of the boats tied up at the Monterey Marina.

Once begun, the traffic thrived. Montalvo bought her place on Carmel Point and lived like a lady of quality, while supervising her operations to the north and south through Farnham and certain trusted—and probably frightened—lieutenants.

When Sheila Lord arrived on the scene, Felicia was hardly aware of it. She had a note from Sheila's mother and promptly forgot about it.

Not until Sheila came knocking timidly at her door did Felicia think about her niece. She gave the young girl tea and dismissed her with a half hour of chilly conversation. Sheila, however, did not perceive the slight and continued dutifully to visit her aunt as a girl

131

of good family would, at least once a month, much to Felicia's disgust.

It was more than a year, as Farnham recalled, before Felicia found a way to use her sister's daughter. The drug traffic through Monterey had been successful, but as word got around among the dealers, the pressure began to grow. Operators in L.A. became conscious of competition from the north. Bits of information had been fed to authorities in Southern California, and the easy flow through Monterey came under surveillance of the federal law. It became more and more difficult to find places to store the merchandise and conduct the business.

"Sheila was so naive, so ingenuous," said Farnham. "Not the most intelligent girl in the world. She had just begun to paint with Farrell and was falling in love with him. When Felicia offered to underwrite her career in art, she was embarrassingly grateful. Her emotional performance filled the old lady with revulsion."

So Felicia installed her niece in a cottage at the Ranch. Sheila was told that it would be necessary from time to time to store very valuable imported merchandise in the house and that the place would be used for high-level business meetings perhaps once a month.

"I rather liked Sheila," Farnham's clear blue eyes grew soft for a moment. "She was a simple, sweet girl with quite a lot of talent for painting. Not especially bright. Often artists aren't. Terrible housekeeper; couldn't cook. Took all of her meals out."

I reacted. "Wait a minute. When I went into that house with the sheriff's men, the kitchen cabinets and shelves were full of cans and packages."

Farnham smiled. "I did that. We stored our goods behind the groceries. We were quite sure that Sheila would never bother to examine the packages. After all, they were Felicia's, and Sheila wouldn't even have thought of opening them. But we were wrong."

The white-haired man had not changed his position during this long conversation. Balestreri and I had remained standing just inside the room. Farnham remained calmly in his full lotus on the tatami mat.

"Sheila's feelings for Farrell got more and more serious. It was not just a physical thing. I don't think the man tried to make her fall in love with him—really, I don't think he gave her much thought at all. But Sheila was obsessed with him—as a lover or, it seemed on occasion, some kind of god. When this became clear, Felicia suggested that I pay a call on Farrell and hint that the romance be terminated. When I suggested what could happen if it were not, Farrell wisely agreed to stop seeing Sheila. She, poor child, became a little unhinged. And, unfortunately, at about the same time, she began to question our activity in her cottage."

Farnham—to my great relief (I was beginning to feel the pain)—grasped an ankle in both hands and gently straightened out one leg and then the other. He sat for a moment with his hands planted on the mat beside him, then stood up slowly and flexed the muscles in his calves. I noticed for the first time that, although he was a relatively small man, he had thick, powerful legs and arms. He turned and looked out through the glass wall into the dark towards the sea.

"One night last February, Sheila, in an especially agitated frame of mind, decided to examine one of our packages. Oh, I don't know if she had suspected all along what we were up to. But she certainly knew—or guessed—what she had found. She was utterly crushed by the discovery. After the loss of Farrell, it was the final blow to learn that her rich, respectable aunt was a criminal. She became hysterical. She piled all her art materials and paintings in the road outside her house, poured turpentine and paint thinner over the lot, and lit a match to it. As the fire became intense, she fed into it fourteen kilos of pure heroin."

A small shudder went through Farnham's body. He stroked his platinum hair with a thin dark hand.

"It represented the loss of a great deal of money. That was bad enough. But it also meant that something had to be done about Sheila. Neither Felicia nor I wished to cope with that disagreeable decision right away. We suspended the drug operation temporarily to allow things to cool down. Sheila went into a mild catatonic state. She saw no one, went out just occasionally—to the grocery for a bit of fruit or to a small restaurant down the road. Actually, she took many meals here with us. But most of the time she stayed in her cottage and read books on metaphysics or watched those ridiculous daytime serials on television. To my knowledge she had only two occasional visitors up to the day of her death: that unstable Blanchard girl from up the hill and an extraordinarily handsome blonde woman whose identity I never learned."

He walked towards the glass wall and placed his hands against it, looking out as if searching for something valuable beyond his reach. His voice was very quiet as he continued.

"The insanity grew deeper. Sheila moved further and further from reality. On the morning of the day of her death, she came here and announced that she was pregnant with the child of a god, and that she had been directed by voices to tell the police what she knew about our drug operation. A sticky situation, you see. We were stunned by the pregnancy. Farrell had been out of the picture—or so we thought—for almost six months. But Nancy Blanchard had taken her to a doctor in Monterey and the pregnancy was a reality. However, when Sheila rambled on about a beautiful dark god who had been coming to her in the night, we got the idea that one or more of the bus boys from the Ranch had happened onto a good thing.

"Sheila's sudden passion for law and order was something else. This we had to deal with immediately."

Farnham turned and faced us, frowning.

"I'll tell you exactly what we thought and what we did. Felicia would cheerfully have had the girl killed. At that point, she might have done it with her own hands. I couldn't see it. Sheila, I thought, could be controlled, could be useful. Maybe I am crueler than Felicia was—just not quite so direct. My suggestion was that we find some way to tie her to us. My method would be to hook her on the heroin we were trading in.

"We made a plan. First, we needed a reason to visit her in the cottage. Didn't want to just barge in and set her off. Felicia thought of a painting we could take her as a sort of peace offering. It was a copy Felicia had made of a nude by Farrell, almost perfect in detail except that—purely out of malice—she had given it Sheila's coloring and deliberately blurred the face. Sheila would recognize

Farrell's style and perhaps be flattered. We really didn't know. At this stage, she was mad. There was no predicting her reaction.

"We went to her place about six. I had phoned her earlier to say that we were indeed sorry that we had used her to hide the drugs, and that we'd like to come and talk it over. She was reluctant in a childlike way because she had arranged to attend a Bach Festival concert with Nancy Blanchard that evening. But I promised her that we would not be long, and she agreed to receive us.

"She seemed pleased with the picture, although she cried when she saw it. She assumed that it was a sort of tribute to her from Farrell, although she told us primly that she had never posed for him. She got a rickety old easel from her bedroom closet—the only thing she hadn't burned, I guess—and displayed the painting on it in the corner of the living room.

"We talked. Felicia was sweet, cajoling, sympathetic, regretful. So sorry about Sheila's unhappiness. Concerned about her health. Did she take vitamins? Poor Sheila took it all in, wide-eyed and believing. She even believed that the injection I put in a vein inside her left elbow was a massive dose of vitamin C."

29

"Ten o'clock. By the nautilus tank."

F ARNHAM'S SHOULDERS sagged. A tear glittered on his cheek. How, I wondered, could this man who had undoubtedly hurt and probably killed people for very little reason—how could he produce a tear? Sense of doom? Fear of death?

He sat on the edge of the high stool I had seen Felicia using on my first visit. He covered his face with one hand.

"That is my story, gentlemen. I do not know who killed Sheila Lord. We left her in a narcotic euphoria. She was wearing a long caftan and lying on her bed, propped up with pillows. It came as rather a shock when they called the following day and told us she was dead."

It had been Farnham who had hit me on the head and had taken the painting and my Polaroid photograph of it. He had arrived ahead of me, opened the door easily with his professional skill, and hid when I bumbled into the house. He apologized—rather nicely I thought. Farnham had a cloak of English middle-class respectability that he could pull round him when he needed it. Balestreri, on the other hand, shot me a sharp glance when he learned that I had been in the cottage that night. But I pushed ahead:

"What about the blood in the painting? I touched it the morning of the murder and it was wet. I checked it just before you slugged me and it was dry. And now it's gone."

"The painting was not as Felicia had painted it. She had not intended it for a chamber of horrors. I brought it to her as it was. She cleaned it and hung it back in the place where it had been. We did not speak of it again."

Farnham looked sadly at Balestreri. "By the by, Sergeant, there is a delivery to be made this morning. At the Monterey Bay Aquarium. Ten o'clock. By the nautilus tank."

"Why are you telling us this?" asked the sergeant.

"Why not?" The white-haired man smiled. "I'm a dead man, Sergeant Balestreri. The Nevada people will know of Felicia's death in hours."

Despite what he had been told, Balestreri made the decision not to arrest Farnham at that time. The man had calmly admitted to a life of criminal activity, but there was no real evidence that could be taken to court. He could still be considered a suspect in the murder of Sheila Lord, but somehow Balestreri and I believed his story. It seemed to both of us that he didn't have a lot to look forward to. We left him sitting hunched on the stool, dwarfed by the great easel, which held a primed canvas ready for another brilliant copy that would never be painted.

When we were out of the house on the sidewalk, Balestreri, who had been uncharacteristically silent, turned to me and said: "Run back in there, Pat, and tell that little creep not to leave town." It was the first time he had used my given name.

I jogged back into the house and ran up the stairs to the studio. Farnham was gone.

Less than a minute had passed, and Farnham was gone. Swiftly I searched the other rooms, but the man had disappeared completely. And judging from what I took to be his own living quarters, he hadn't even taken his toothbrush.

I sat down on a chair in the hallway to catch my breath. What a damn shame that I should be doing all that work for nothing. With a rush of righteous indignation, I dashed up the stairs to the studio and swiped...the tatami mat.

When I appeared at Balestreri's car with the bundle under my arm, he pretended not to notice.

"The guy was gone, Sergeant. Into thin air. I looked all over the house."

"Not to worry, Riordan. They'll get him. They always do."

I stuffed the mat into the back seat and slid into the car. Balestreri sat quietly for a few moments before he spoke.

"Well, Riordan, we know an awful lot, don't we? We know about Miss Montalvo's untimely demise. That has to be put down as a hit and run for the moment. Or some business rival had her moves figured out, and hit her at the right time in the right place. Either way, she's out of it. Maybe just death by a drunk in a pickup truck. Maybe the guy didn't even realize he hit something.

"We know much more about Sheila Lord. The girl was having trouble with her head. She was pregnant by person or persons unknown who materialized in the dead of night. She was full of dope because Farnham shot it into her.

"Only one thing we don't know, right? We don't know who made a hole in her throat and let her bleed to death."

I don't remember exactly what time it was when Balestreri dropped me off at my car in the parking lot at the beach. He carefully turned his head away as I transferred my stolen goods from the sheriff's car to the trunk of the Mercedes. I don't know to this day why I took the tatami mat. I justify the crime by convincing myself that it was a souvenir for Reiko, something for her to sit on when she felt very, very Japanese.

"Oh, Riordan. I'm going to call Al McManus, and we're going to meet Farnham's delivery boy at the aquarium. Place opens at nine-thirty in the summer. If you want to join us, I'll pick you up around nine, OK?"

"I'm your man, Sergeant." It was early in the morning yet, and I needed a cup of coffee very much.

30

"Do you know how many members of the Screen Actors Guild there are in southern California?"

THE MONTEREY BAY Aquarium was built by a rich man for his marine biologist daughter. Papa had made one of the world's largest fortunes as a Silicon Valley pioneer and felt, I guess, that he owed the public something for helping to computerize the world.

The place takes up all of the space formerly occupied by the last functioning cannery on that little strip of coastland along Monterey Bay immortalized by Steinbeck as Cannery Row.

The computer magnate's offspring has done a magnificent job. The aquarium is impressive, innovatively designed, and well stocked with marine life, mainly from Monterey Bay. It has attracted a constant stream of visitors since it opened, and the line to get into the place is often two blocks long.

Parking is murder. The lots of a supermarket and a couple of fast food restaurants nearby are plastered with large signs warning aquarium visitors to keep out or be towed away. But I can't figure out how they tell who's who.

Balestreri had no problem. He drove the sheriff's car onto aquarium property up to the members' entrance and left it there. McManus had arrived earlier, and was pacing back and forth before the doors.

We huddled momentarily before entering the building.

"You know this place?" asked Balestreri of the federal man.

"I've been here with my kids, but there must have been a thousand people inside, and I don't remember much."

The sergeant turned to me. "Well, Riordan?"

"The chambered nautiluses are tucked away in a corner somewhere on the ground level. They don't pull a big crowd like the sea otters or the Monterey Bay tank or the places where the kids can handle the animals.

"But listen, this guy is probably going to be dressed differently from last time, and hard to spot. I think I have a good notion of his face. If he sees the three of us together, he'll suspect something and take off in a hurry. I'll move in alone because I look more like a tourist and less like a cop. You guys hang back."

We marched in past the gate guard, Balestreri and McManus flashing their ID's, sandwiching me in between. I took the lead and walked quickly under the fiberglass whales, past the sea otters, past the Monterey Bay tank and around to a comparatively quiet corner where I knew the tank for the chambered nautilus was. It is one of the two creatures in the aquarium that does not even pay an occasional visit to Monterey Bay. It lives in the depths of the southeastern Pacific and has remained essentially unchanged, scientists say, for 450 million years. It's also the only animal here that's had a poem written about it, although the experts say that Oliver Wendell Holmes had very little knowledge of the beast. The other stranger to the bay, a late arrival, is the cuttlefish, whose main claim to fame is that it secretes a fluid called sepia which gave its name to a color.

I tried to look like your ordinary tourist who'd just waited an hour in line and paid seven bucks to get in. I dawdled in front of adjacent exhibits, keeping a careful watch for the man with the goods. I was only sure that he wouldn't turn up as an old salt with a picnic basket.

Then he was there, approaching the nautilus tank from my right, paler than before, dressed this time in a natty yachtsman's cap, a perfectly fitting blue blazer with white trousers, an open collar with a foulard ascot, and on his feet, expensive deck shoes. He was carrying a large camera bag.

I signalled Balestreri and McManus.

We moved in and pinned the man against the glass of the tank.

"Oh, my God," he said in a deep, resonant voice. Then he wrenched free, ducked under our arms, and dived into the crowd.

We shoved aside a dozen flabbergasted fish-watchers and caught sight of him as he rounded a bank of display tanks and made for the entrance of the aquarium. He was a chunky man and he moved with unexpected speed. Balestreri was shouting with a voice of command, and the aquarium security guards responded by sealing off the exits.

Our man was in a panic. He stopped near the main entrance and ran back directly at us, like a halfback suddenly cutting back against the flow of traffic. I lunged at him as he went by but all I got hold of was an innocent tourist.

On went the counterfeit yachtsman, clutching his camera bag for dear life. Up the stairs to the second level from which there is no exit. Frantically, he ran, stopped, ran again. Finally, as if looking for an end to his misery, he pushed aside a lady with a small child in a stroller, and found himself in a small gallery on the second level of a seabird sanctuary.

McManus, Balestreri, and I burst in almost simultaneously. The man leaned against the railing of the gallery, breathing heavily. He was in a heavy sweat and his make-up was running. His eyes darted about, looking for an escape route. Then, with a little cry, he fell over backwards into the wet terrain of the bird sanctuary, landed on his feet, and rolled slowly over on his back with the camera bag held tightly to his chest.

He lay there with his eyes closed. The birds were quite naturally disturbed and flew squawking to the top of the sanctuary. Two or three of the aquarium guards surrounded the quarry, and the three of us came down the stairs.

We fished the miserable fellow out of the water. He wasn't hurt—if you don't count his pride and a bruised fanny. I took the camera bag. Balestreri and McManus each clamped an arm and walked the dripping man in silence out of the aquarium. His nice new expensive deck shoes left neat prints across the floor.

Balestreri hustled the man into the back seat of the sheriff's car and pushed in next to him. McManus entered from the other side. I slid into the driver's seat.

The camera bag, of course, contained no camera. Only bags of white powder which McManus identified immediately as heroin by cutting a hole in one bag and tasting a small amount. I have always meant to ask one of these experts just what heroin is supposed to taste like, but I missed another opportunity.

Our man was, as I had suspected, an out-of-work actor.

"Do you know how many members of the Screen Actors Guild there are in southern California? And how many aren't working? Well, Patty Duke is doing the best she can, I guess. But she's already got hers, and the rest of us are still. . . ." He fell silent, contemplating the end of a less than brilliant career. He'd needed the work. A guy in a bar in Santa Monica offered him work. All he'd have to do was deliver stuff off a small yacht, making sure he created a different character for each delivery. Just deliver stuff once a week in Monterey.

He told us all he knew. He had met Farnham, of course, but was unaware of the old lady. He had some key contacts in Los Angeles and a code name for his source in Mexico. McManus nodded as the actor spilled his guts. All the characters were known to the feds.

What boat did he come in on? Well, that's pretty funny. The actor's transportation was a slick little motor yacht called *The Pumpkin Eater* that some years ago had belonged to—would you believe—George Spelvin. I had helped him name it. You know, "had a wife and couldn't keep her." George had problems trying to navigate while drunk, and the Coast Guard had suggested he get rid of it.

So now the government has it. And Felicia Montalvo's territory is open for the opportunist.

Balestreri dropped me off at my house before hauling his prisoner over to Salinas to the county jail.

31

I couldn't get her out of my mind.

WHEN THE sergeant dropped me off at my cottage, I was tired but strung out. I took a shower, put on fresh clothes, and opened a can of soup for lunch. I get pretty tired of eating out at Carmel prices. the promise of a bright warm day.

Something was eating at my gut that wouldn't go away, something I didn't want to think about. I walked out into the sun's warmth and got in the car. I didn't want to go to the office, I didn't want to see anybody, I just wanted to think. And I think better in my little Mercedes.

I was depressed. Despite the excitement at the aquarium, the emotional experiences of the morning and the night before had me confused. Not since I got out of the army after Korea and plunged into a strange, placid, self-satisfied world, had I been so terribly confused.

You don't fall in love with a woman in a couple of days. You feel lust for a beautiful woman with a good body, yes. You admire a woman with a good mind and a fine sense of humor, yes. But you don't fall in love.

And yet—I was driving through the Carmel Highlands and the road twisted and turned. I had driven this stretch of road hundreds of times. The car was on automatic pilot. My mind was full of questions.

When I got around to admitting it to myself, it seemed pretty foolish. Helen used to call me "the last of the great romantics." What was it really about Debbie Spelvin?

After all, her husband had hired me to check up on her. She had been involved—more or less innocently, she claimed—with two of my friends. She had what you might call a checkered past. She fell into my bed rather hastily, I thought. I couldn't get her out of my mind.

I remember reading something that a psychiatrist said about being in love. If the object of your affection is in your thoughts more than a certain percentage of the time, you can be said "to be in love." "To love," on the other hand, is an entirely different thing. It takes time and understanding. I loved Helen; I guess I was in love with Debbie. Maybe "infatuated," with its implication of foolishness, was a better word. Maybe I could love her in the other way with time. But I was doubtful about her feelings for me.

By this time, the road had leveled out and the Pacific spread to my right. It was a deep blue in the bright sunshine. I passed Greg Farrell's place and remembered my visit earlier in the week. Debbie in the tight, faded jeans and the bulky navy sweater, her silky blonde hair mussed by the ocean breeze.

Just before you get to the first big bridge is a pullout for sightseers. There are many of these wide places on this road. There are many sights to see. But this one features a huge rock perched on the edge of a sheer drop that must be more than four hundred feet. I pulled off the road and parked near the rock.

As I sat, I thought, "That's me, there. That big rock on the verge of going over the cliff. I had better be goddam careful."

I'm not sure how long I sat there, playing with my thoughts. Quite a while, I'd guess. The sun was moving towards the western horizon and the daylight was beginning to take on a shade of gold.

The empty feeling was still there as I drove back up the road towards Carmel. The day trippers were pouring out of Point Lobos as I passed. The night seemed to be coming on very quickly.

I drove over to Monterey to a place on Cannery Row where a

jazz combo played nightly. It annoyed the waiter that I drank nothing but mineral water, and it annoyed me that I had to pay three bucks a pop for it. Feeling guilty, I left the poor bastard a big tip.

The animal has to be fed. On the trip back over the hill to Carmel, I got a craving for food, so I stopped at a pizza parlor and bought a medium combination with anchovies which I took home and devoured, secure in the knowledge that the nightmares it might produce couldn't be any worse than the one I had been living for a number of days.

When I woke up the next morning, my left eye was stuck shut, and I had a nasty sinus headache. It had turned clammy cold, and I had left the windows open. I unstuck my eye with my left thumb and forefinger and peered out the window into the chill gray dawn.

32

"She is a passionate lady, Pat."

I T HAD BEEN a trying time. I had moved into the house in Carmel, established my office in Monterey, looking forward to the serenity of the fog, the good restaurants, the art galleries, the old friends. But Carmel-by-the-Sea, a place which had always before had a tranquilizing effect on me, had provided me with more excitement than I ever really wanted.

I sat on the edge of my bed, bleary-eyed and unshaven, staring out the window at the big red dog who always seemed to be staring back at me. I should paint that good animal, I thought. He's got such a great color, and he's so calm and dignified.

As I sat, clutching the edge of the bed and wondering whether to get up or just roll back and pull the covers over my head, the germ of an idea began to grow in the back of my mind. I needed just one more answer to one more very important question. With it, I might be able, I thought, to make the pieces of the puzzle come together.

It was after ten when I arrived at Armand Colbert's Carmel restaurant. The place doesn't serve breakfast (like Chinese restaurants, remember?) and the lunch service doesn't begin until eleven-thirty.

I had reasoned earlier that Armand could help me in my inquiries about Sheila Lord. He'd had a strange reaction when I had mentioned Debbie Spelvin. But now I knew that he and Debbie had been more than casual acquaintances.

149

Armand Colbert is a remarkably gifted man. In the years that I have known him, he has never failed at anything he has tried.

Maybe it has to do with how he arrived in this world. He was born in the basement of a ruined house in a village near Malmedy, Belgium, in January of 1945 while the Ardennes Offensive (we called it the "Battle of the Bulge") was going on all around him.

Armand and his family, like many in his country, were left with nothing—nothing but indomitable spirit. They survived and flourished. The spirit and energy of the Colberts carried over to this country when they arrived as immigrants in the late fifties.

Musician, artist, craftsman, businessman—Armand has been the star of the family. My only quarrel with him is that he stopped painting. Just stopped, cold turkey. A gift simply cast away.

"I lost interest," he said when I asked him. "I may begin again."

But he never has. He bought a house up the hill and added a big wing to it, part of which was to contain a studio. But he has never picked up a brush since he "lost interest."

He's sort of an Alexander, always looking for new worlds to conquer. He runs three restaurants now, and all the other family interests. His vineyard in the Cachagua Valley, sheltered from the coastal fog, has produced its first grapes. And he plans a chateau on the vineyard land, a place of quiet for guests who want rest and relaxation as well as good food and wine. Guests whose credit ratings match George Spelvin's.

He always has beautiful women around him, but seems not to hear when questioned about marriage. He dotes on his nieces and nephews and spoils them whenever he can. He exudes irresistible European charm that comes as naturally as breathing.

I found Armand where I thought I would, sitting at a small table at the back of the patio, examining the previous day's receipts. He greeted me pleasantly enough but he was just a shade annoyed, I think, that I had interrupted his conduct of business.

He gave me a nervous smile. "Have some coffee, Pat. Maybe a waffle. A little juice. Piece of fruit. Everything is fresh, you know."

I accepted the coffee and politely declined the food. There was still an echo of anchovies from the very late pizza of the night before. Allowing only the minimum courtesy of small talk, I went right to the point.

"Armand, the last time I saw you, you got very upset when I mentioned Debbie Spelvin's name. Why?"

His eyes narrowed and he sat up very stiffly in his straight-backed chair. He thought for a long moment, and when he spoke, it was clear that he had chosen his words carefully.

"She is in love with Greg Farrell, Pat. Or violently infatuated. Now, that doesn't bother me in itself. Greg is an attractive man. She is a beautiful woman. A little older than she would have you believe, you understand. But that is sometimes a rather endearing female characteristic. Yes, she is beautiful, but somewhat—unstable."

He fumbled for just the right words. "I was very close to her for a while. When she married George and came to live in Pebble Beach, she soon became a familiar—vision around town, with or without her husband. They came here often. You know George. George likes to drink. After a couple of months, he would frequently leave the table before dessert and wander off. Several times I had to drive the lady home. Later she came in regularly alone. We became good friends. Good friends.

"She is a passionate lady, Pat. And totally captivating. I have had some little experience with women—as you know—but this one was almost more than I could handle. Then I made a mistake. I introduced her to Greg. One could immediately feel the electricity. I knew that my time had passed, but I think I am not yet over it."

I understand, Armand—God, do I ever understand. He seemed to have forgotten the dinner checks he had been tabulating, and stared at me for a moment.

"She took up oil painting only so she could study with Greg. She has no gift, not the slightest. She...*smears*. She bought the most expensive brushes and paints with George's money. Her representational work has no balance, no perspective, no color sense; her abstracts lack both feeling and intelligence. The only tool she approaches using well is the palette knife. She seems to enjoy laying on the pigments as a bricklayer spreads mortar."

My adrenaline began to flow. I clumsily excused myself to

Armand and left the restaurant at a dead run. I stopped only to use the pay phone at the Shell station on the corner to leave a message for Sergeant Balestreri.

In five minutes I was winding along the Seventeen Mile Drive. I had paid the money at the gate to avoid the guard's phoning ahead. I really didn't want Debbie to know I was coming.

33

"Sublimation for the baser drives."

SHE ANSWERED my ring herself, as she had on my previous visit. Only this time, she just let the door swing open and looked at me vacantly. She was wearing a loose smock, spotted with paint, and she stood with her hands thrust deep in its pockets.

"Hello, Pat." Her voice was dull.

It was if it had never happened. Two nights before, I had made love to this woman, and now I seemed to be looking at a total stranger.

"Hello, Debbie. George here?"

"Nobody's here. Just me. I'm nobody. Maybe that's the way you wanted it, huh?" She was trying to smile.

I ignored the question. "You've been painting."

"You're right, Pat, I've been painting. I can't paint worth a damn. I suppose somebody's already told you that. But it's therapy. I like to spread the colors around. Like peanut butter."

"Can we have a talk?"

"Sure. Come on in. You can come upstairs and watch me paint."

Debbie's studio was bright and pleasant—a converted bedroom—and much smaller than Felicia Montalvo's. Her paintings, scattered around the room, were very bad. Not promising, not primitive. Just bad.

The canvas she had been working on was on an easel facing the windows in the north wall. She had apparently laid on a thick black undercoat and was applying strips of color with a palette knife.

"Why did you come to me the other night, Debbie? Not for a confession. I'm sure as hell not a priest."

She was squeezing a line of bright yellow paint onto a paper palette.

"I needed what you had, Riordan, that's all. I needed to be loved."

She carefully replaced the cap on the tube of paint. "What's it all about, Riordan?" she asked casually as she stroked the blade of the palette knife across the canvas.

"Just to clear my mind, Debbie, I'd like to ask you a couple of questions."

"OK. Don't know how I can help you—but go ahead."

"You told me that you visited Sheila on the afternoon of her murder, right?"

"Right. I used to drop in on her once or twice a week. Of course, you know that she was, well, very depressed during the last few months."

"How long did you stay?"

"An hour—maybe a little more. She told me her aunt was coming about six and that she was going to a concert with Nancy Blanchard that evening. I left about five."

"That was the last time you saw her?"

"Yes, of course."

"Did...did she tell you anything while you were there? About herself?"

Debbie's grip tightened just a little on the palette knife, and the careful yellow line she was making wavered.

"Nothing special."

"She didn't tell you she was pregnant—by Greg Farrell?"

The knife stopped. Debbie put it down carefully on the small table that held her paints.

"What are you driving at, Riordan?"

"Well, you two were such good friends. I thought she might have given you the news. You know, one girl to another."

Debbie's body was rigid under the flowing smock. There was a tremor in her hand as she picked up the palette knife again.

"The...poor thing...she had so many quirks, so many illusions.

She did tell me. I just wrote it off as another crazy idea. Greg hadn't even seen her for months, I knew. I think I know what you're suggesting, Riordan. No chance. She was alive and in good spirits when I left."

She was not looking at me. She was squinting at her canvas, perhaps visualizing her painting, perhaps avoiding my eyes.

"Where did you go when you left Sheila?"

"Why, home—here. It was the cocktail hour, Riordan. And I thought I just might catch my husband if, by chance, he had torn himself away from the bar at the Lodge. As it happens, I didn't. He didn't come home until after two in the morning. You know, when all the saloons are closed."

"You spent the evening at home?"

"Yes. Had a drink, had a sandwich, and came up here to paint. Therapy, Riordan. Sublimation for the baser drives."

She had relaxed a little when we got past the business of Sheila's pregnancy. The palette knife was busy again, spreading heavy horizontal bands of thick primary color.

"Debbie, Greg told me you called him about nine o'clock on that night." The knife stopped in mid-stroke.

"I...I did. Although I knew that poor Sheila was just crazy... I...had to talk to Greg...to make sure. I only talked to him a short while. He assured me that Sheila's baby was not his. That's all."

"Then the idea that Sheila's affair with Farrell might have continued even while he was romancing you...that's what had you pretty upset?"

She turned that lovely face towards me and I could see the tiny muscles twitching at the corners of her mouth. A vein swelled in her forehead like a segmented, pulsing worm. Her eyes widened, the white showing all around. Her grip tightened on the palette knife and she took a step towards me.

"You sonofabitch! You cheap sonofabitch, you are accusing *me*! What do you think you have on me? What do you think you can make me do or say?"

I knew I had her completely off balance. I had to make her fall.

"I want you to tell me just how—and why—you killed Sheila Lord."

She was on me like a cat, and I just managed to see the knife blade falling in a multi-colored arc. I caught a glancing blow with my left forearm and grabbed her wrist with my right hand. An experienced knee got me in the groin, but a little off center. I twisted the palette knife out of her hand and put her out with a right to the point of the jaw that sent a sharp pain through my hand. The painting was jarred from the easel and fell face down, printing a crazy rainbow on her smock.

The inevitable conclusion.

34

*"I'm not going out with a bang.
Just a whimper..."*

I ASKED A friend of mine—a Chinese who grew up on Grant
Avenue in San Francisco—why Chinese restaurants never serve
breakfast.

He looked at me, incredulous. "They *do*, Pat. The ones where the
Chinese go. Not the big white-tablecloth joints like Kan's or the
Imperial Palace. But the little places on the side streets. Hell,
Chinese people have to eat in the morning like everybody else."

For a while that kind of spoiled the little notion that Helen and I
had dreamed up so many years ago. Still, I haven't seen one yet
myself. That is, a Chinese restaurant that serves breakfast. And when
I asked my friend what the Chinese eat in the morning, he told me
that his own breakfast never varies: a fried egg chopped up in a bowl
of rice and doused with oyster sauce. But then he has always
claimed to have been a tough Grant Avenue kid. The fact is, he's a
high school biology teacher, and he stretches the truth a bit. Besides,
how many people are going to go to breakfast in a place that serves
chopped fried eggs in rice, smothered with oyster sauce?

But there's no denying that the conclusion was inevitable, the
condition immutable. The lady I thought I was in love with was a
killer.

I sat on the floor in that cluttered studio beside the unconscious
woman who had come to mean so much to me. A dull ache began

157

in the middle of my chest. I felt tears welling up in my eyes. How could it have happened to me? I don't wear my heart on my sleeve. I am practical—even cynical—about emotional attachments. With Helen it was sort of matter-of-fact, although our devotion to each other was deep and genuine. And I love Reiko in a certain way, limited by a tacit agreement that we can only be best friends.

Debbie's eyes fluttered and opened. She looked up at me and said quietly, "You didn't have to hit me so hard, you bastard."

There was no anger in her face or her voice. She closed her eyes and inhaled deeply as she rubbed her jaw with a paint-stained hand, leaving small yellow streaks on her chin.

"You would have killed me if you could have, honey."

"I don't think so, Riordan. You're one of the old-fashioned good guys, remember? I couldn't kill you. I'm not going out with a bang. Just a whimper, a faint whimper."

"What happened, Debbie?"

I put a pillow under her head. She closed her eyes again.

"Sheila told me about her pregnancy. I wrote it off, just as I told you. But when I got home, it was bugging me. It grew in my head. I began asking myself if it was possible. That's when I called Greg.

"He was pretty short with me on the phone. Not cruel, just impatient. He denied having anything to do with Sheila for nearly half a year. I believed him.

"Then Sheila called me. She sounded doped up...but she got that way sometimes. Sort of incoherent. She talked about how proud she was about the baby, and sorry for me because she knew I liked Greg.

"Something snapped, Riordan. I drove down to her cottage. She was in bed, propped up with pillows, singing some crazy tune. She kept talking like she had on the phone, crazy, disconnected. I couldn't stand it. I got up and went into the living room. And there was that painting I could swear was Greg's.

"I was furious. I dragged Sheila from the bed and hauled her into the living room.

"She stood, swaying back and forth in front of the painting, laughing hysterically.

"I lost control completely. I had an eight-inch palette knife in the pocket of my smock, and I pulled it out and went after her. I don't think I meant to kill her. Just hurt her, cut her, make her stop laughing. Sheila fell backwards onto the chaise longue, and I fell on top of her. She didn't really resist or make any noise when I pushed that palette knife into her throat.

"I pulled off her caftan and watched the blood flow out of her.

"Then I realized that the painting wasn't complete."

When Balestreri arrived, Debbie was still on the floor.

"What do I take her in for, Riordan?"

"She killed Sheila Lord. She just told me. If that isn't enough, you can take her in for assault with a deadly weapon. I'll sign a complaint."

35

"You could kill somebody like that with a sharp pencil."

How'd she do it, Riordan?"

Balestreri was driving us over to Salinas to book Debbie into the county jail. She was in the back seat with me. I held her with her head on my shoulder, and she seemed to sleep. That happens to people sometimes when they finally get a big burden off their backs.

"She did it with a palette knife, Sergeant. Bad thing for a murder weapon. Not really sharp, pretty flexible. But if the victim doesn't resist—and Sheila *was* full of heroin. You could kill somebody like that with a sharp pencil."

In Salinas, they booked Debbie for Murder One. It'd probably go to second degree, maybe even manslaughter. Balestreri had me sign an ADW complaint just to be safe.

"Rich people get good lawyers," he said.

George Spelvin loved her and he most certainly was rich.

The sergeant drove me back to the Spelvin place in Pebble Beach to pick up my car. On the way, he and I went over all of the details of this bizarre case. So many angles.

Felicia Montalvo was obviously the Monterey County drug connection. Greg Farrell, while a Don Juan of considerable skill, was entirely innocent. Sheila's pregnancy was real, but probably the result of an encounter with an opportunistic bus boy from the Ranch restaurant. Sheila, poor thing, was vulnerable, very vulnerable. The Blanchards would emerge unscathed and live unhappily ever after, although I held out some hope for Nancy. Raul Jimenez would be reunited with his family, and Adele would keep him on the payroll. Armand Colbert, whom Debbie regarded as the most charming man she knew, would remain a very good restaurateur.

"Wait a minute, Riordan. What about the painting? You went through all that business about its being wet, and dry, and cleaned up. What was that all about? It had been painted quite a long time before the murder."

"Oh, Debbie did that. Her final touch. She thought the painting ought to duplicate the scene."

"You mean she brought paint with her, too? I know there wasn't any art stuff around the house."

"No, Tony. Debbie didn't bring any paint. She improvised with the nearest thing at hand. Sheila Lord's blood. Laid on with a palette knife."

That's why the stuff was tacky in the morning and dry the next day, flaking off under my touch. Felicia Montalvo must have known. It probably washed off with a damp cloth. Maybe that's what Felicia was thinking about when the pickup sent her to death on the rocks.

Balestreri and I said goodbye in front of George Spelvin's big ugly house. I promised to be on tap for the trial, whenever it might come.

On my way out, I passed George's car weaving slowly along the road. I shouted at him when he swerved at me, driving me over the shoulder and twenty feet onto the rough of the Spyglass Hill Golf Course. But I didn't want to talk to him just then. Fortunately, he didn't recognize me—just stared straight ahead, clutching the wheel with the painful concentration of the truly drunk.

I thought about Helen. She would have appreciated the ironies of my adventure. I thought of Reiko. She would cluck and scold, and I simply would not tell her about my night with Debbie Spelvin.

I thought about Debbie. A lady abandoned by fortune. It got to be just too much for her. I am still sentimental enough to think that at another time, in another place... maybe things could have been a lot different.

Coming out of the Seventeen Mile Drive into Carmel, I turned up Ocean Avenue. It was dark. There are no street lights in Carmel. I took a left on Dolores and found a place to park on Fifth near the post office. There's a Chinese restaurant across the street.

When the waiter brought my cashew chicken and ginger beef, I looked up at him:

"You serve breakfast?"

Clearly, he thought I was crazy, and quickly he walked away.

About the Author

Roy Gilligan has been a radio-TV personality, a newspaper columnist, and a teacher. He has written for the *San Francisco Chronicle, San Jose Mercury-News, Monterey Peninsula Herald, San Francisco Focus,* and Whodunnit Productions, among many others. Mr. Gilligan lives in San Jose, California, with his wife of thirty-seven years. He has one daughter and fond memories of four of the nicest dogs that ever lived.

About the Publisher

Perseverance Press publishes a new line of old-fashioned mysteries. Emphasis is on the classic whodunit, with no excessive gore, exploitive sex, or gratuitous violence.

#1 *DEATH SPIRAL, Murder at the Winter Olympics* $6.95
by Meredith Phillips (1984)

It's a cold war on ice as love and defection breed murder at the winter Olympics. Who killed world champion skater Dima Kuznetsov, the "playboy of the Eastern world": old or new lovers, hockey right-wingers, jealous rivals, the KGB? Will skating sleuth Lesley Grey discover the murderer before she herself is hunted down?

Reviews said: "fair without being easy to solve" *(Drood Review),* "strongly recommended" (BBC Radio), "timely and topical" (Allen Hubin), "appealing" *(Oakland Tribune),* "surprises, suspense, and a truly unusual murder method" (Marvin Lachman), "informative and entertaining" (Carol Brener), "Olympics buffs and skating fans will appreciate the frequent chats about sports-lore and Squaw Valley history" *(Kirkus Reviews).*

Not recommended for under 16 years of age.

#2 *TO PROVE A VILLAIN* $6.95
by Guy M. Townsend (1985)

No one has solved this mystery in five centuries: was King Richard III responsible for the smothering of his nephews, the little Princes in the Tower of London?

Now, a modern-day murderer stalks a quiet college town, claiming victims in the same way. When the beautiful chairman of the English department dies, John Forest, a young history professor beset by personal and romantic problems, must grapple with both mysteries. Then he learns he may be next on the killer's list. . . .

Reviews said: "a mystery set in academe that's wonderfully free from pedantry or stuffiness *(ALA booklist)*, "most ingenious" (John Ball), "a tight, fast-paced tale" *(Louisville Courier-Journal)*, "a daring undertaking" *(San Jose Mercury)*, "lucid and very well-written" *(Midwest Book Review)*, "nicely constructed and unfailingly interesting" (Jon L. Breen), "entertaining and illuminating" (Allen Hubin, *Ellery Queen's Mystery Magazine*).

TO ORDER: Add $1.05 to your check for retail price to cover shipping for each of these quality paperbacks.

Mail to:
    Perseverance Press
    P.O. Box 384
    Menlo Park, California 94026

California residents please add 6½% tax (45¢ per book at $6.95 and 52¢ per book at $7.95).

#3 *PLAY MELANCHOLY BABY* $7.95
by John Daniel (1986)

Murder most Californian: murder *in* the hot tub, murder *with* the wine bottle, murder *by*. . .?

When the obnoxious piano player is discovered floating face down with a fractured skull, no one has a Clue whodunit. Casey has his hands full already, what with his job (playing old songs in a new world) and new and old loves, not to mention thugs of various nationalities who keep popping up.

But the past won't stay dead. When he finds himself in hot water as prime suspect and/or next victim, he realizes it's time to play Sam Spade and dig up some clues. And all he knows for sure is that it wasn't Col. Mustard.

Reviews said: "Daniel's wry wit and deft plotting alleviate much of the melancholy in a mystery that moves to the rhythms of a different music. That difference, coupled with the character study at the heart of the novel, makes fine reading." (Howard Lachtman, *San Francisco Chronicle Review*). "Readers will thoroughly enjoy the engaging first-person narrative, snappy dialogue, and references to popular music *(ALA booklist)*. "Hip, stylish, and self-confident; a very good mystery novel." *(Santa Cruz Sentinel)*. "I suggest that you 'linger awhile' with this one, for 'this is a lovely way to spend an evening.' "*(Santa Barbara Magazine)*.

Not recommended for under 16 years of age.

#4 *CHINESE RESTAURANTS NEVER SERVE* $7.95
BREAKFAST
by Roy Gilligan (1986)

There's an epidemic with 27 million victims. And no visible symptoms.

It's an epidemic of people who can't read.

Believe it or not, 27 million Americans are functionally illiterate, about one adult in five.

The solution to this problem is you... when you join the fight against illiteracy. So call the Coalition for Literacy at toll-free **1-800-228-8813** and volunteer.

**Volunteer
Against Illiteracy.
The only degree you need
is a degree of caring.**

Ad Council Coalition for Literacy